"Bravo to my fellow Arkansan. Her book is honest and it's real. It is sure to resonate with readers."

Celia Anderson

Author of *Love, Ocean and Daddy's Home*

www.celiaanderson.com

"Do not conform any longer to the pattern of the world, but be transformed by the renewing of your mind..."

Romans 12:2

MAMA, YOU'RE CRAZY

Patricia Corcoran
&
Ashleigh Corcoran Weiss

Emerald Ink Publishing
Hot Springs, Arkansas

ISBN 978-1-885373-69-4

Printed in the United States of America

ACKNOWLEDGMENTS

*I*n loving memory of Roger L. Heflin, Jacqeline McCracken Campbell and L. Spanky Hambrick. You left me far too soon and I miss you every day that I live.

Thank you to my brother, Stan and his wife Sandy. Your encouragement and advice are invaluable. I love you and thank you for always being there for me.

Thank you to my brother, Paul, whose assistance saved me great embarrassment. I cherish our relationship.

For my sister, Mary, for your constant love and friendship.

To my dear friend, Carolyn Porter, forever loyal, believing in me and pushing me. Thank you.

Thank you, my sweet, witty daughter, Ashleigh Corcoran Weiss. You share this book with me. I couldn't have done it without your input and help. You bring me constant joy and laughter.

Thank you to my dear friend, Gail Mortensen. We birthed our baby daughters together, Ashleigh and Shannon. You can't get any closer than that.

Thank you to Chris Carson, my agent who has become my friend. I appreciate your help and encouragement.

PERSONAL DISCLAIMER

I believe in total honesty (except in certain situations where someone would be unnecessarily hurt — me, for instance). However, when I began this book, my penchant for honesty flew right out the window. So trust me when I vow to you, every thing in this book is a pack of lies.

1

"*S*weetie, I'm so glad you're here! I'm afraid I've gotten myself into a little mess, and I just don't know where to go from here."

"Mama, it's the middle of the night! Couldn't whatever this is have waited 'til morning?" Savannah was losing patience with her mother. She'd practiced her impatience while driving over from her own house. "Honey, I wish it could. Now, just come upstairs with me. I need you to check on the Senator."

"Something's wrong with Buddy?" Now, Savannah was more worried than impatient.

"Well, sweetie, I'm afraid your step-daddy might've taken a few too many of his pills, you know, the ones for his nerves?" Sadie, Savannah's more than eccentric mother, was acting a bit uncomfortable—or so it seemed to Savannah.

"Why do you think that, Mama?"

Sadie looked away. "Well, I may have put too many of them in his drink."

"Oh God! Have you killed him, Mama?" Savannah was practically screaming at her mother. Sadie drew back and became an inch taller. Savannah started running toward her mother's bedroom.

"Of course I haven't killed him! Why would you say such a thing? Good God! You are so judgmental!"

They were upstairs by this time, in Buddy and Sadie's conjugal bedroom. At least the one they shared on occasion. There were several bedrooms in the house.

Where they slept depended upon the level of the most recent abominable act committed by one or the other. The proximity of the bedroom chosen by either was in direct relation to the degree of anger they were feeling at the moment. It was complicated. And, it was a big house. "My God, Mama! He looks dead!" Savannah rushed to Buddy's bedside and felt his pulse.

"Hell, he always looks dead, Savannah." Sadie folded her arms and looked heavenward, obviously bored with this drama.

"Okay, Mama, he's not dead, but he barely has a pulse." Savannah conceded.

"You're exaggerating, angel."

Savannah appeared to be working herself into a frenzy.

"What if he's in a coma? I think he is, Mama, he's in a coma. You've gone too far this time, Mama. I swear to God— I'm going to have a breakdown because of you and your insane antics."

Savannah was close to hysteria. Sadie couldn't stand this. She lived for Savannah—always had. Sadie had put Savannah on a pedestal that went far beyond any human's ability to reach, much less sustain.

Sadie was crushed because Savannah was so angry with her. But she still had enough spunk to protect herself, even from her beloved daughter.

Damn it to hell! Why had she even called Savannah?

"Oh, for God's sake, Savannah. I was married to a doctor and I've had two years of nurse's training. I can tell the difference between a drug induced coma and a deep sleep. I haven't killed him! Forevermore, child, you act like I'm some sort of criminal."

"Mama, his pulse is weak and you admitted you gave him too much of his medicine."

"Well, he got so damned riled up over the television news. Frankly, I thought he was going to work himself into a heart attack. I did it to calm him down. Probably saved his sorry life." Sadie said this with no small amount of pride.

Savannah looked at her mother, fascinated and horrified. She doesn't see anything wrong with what she's done, Savannah realized.

"Mama, you've got to call an ambulance and get him to the hospital."

"Damn it, Savannah! He'll be fine. I'll call his doctor in the morning and he can determine what should be done. Shit! That's what I should have done to start with.

"But, go comb your hair and put on a little makeup in case we do have to call someone. What time did you say it was? Never mind, it's settled, I'll call Dr. Rush in the morning. You just go on home, honey." Savannah was fuming. All she had heard was her mother suggesting she make herself 'presentable'. She looked at her mother standing there in her adorable short blond (highlighted) hairdo, the ever-present three carat diamond stud earrings—well, she couldn't criticize those—Sadie had given Savannah an identical pair and Savannah was rarely without them.

Her mother's makeup was perfect. Did she go to bed that way? In case of fire? Or a husband's impending death?

Savannah came back to her anger.

"I'm *not* going to brush my hair or put on any makeup! Damn it to hell, Mama, you called me over here in the middle of the night to do my makeup? You may have killed your husband!"

"Oh, Savannah, don't be so dramatic. You said yourself you felt a pulse. I hadn't thought he had a pulse for years."

"Mama! What the hell's wrong with you?"

"Don't sass your mama, baby girl. Now, come on, lighten up. You need to laugh more. You're so pretty when you laugh. Now, don't you go turning into one of those hateful, bitter women. You've always been so much fun, and you're so pretty. Why do you fight me so on wearing makeup?"

Savannah's nostrils flared.

"Kiss my velvet white ass, Lady Sadie! I'm not going to make myself presentable. Presentation is not my big hang-up, it's yours! I'm going to sit right here by Buddy's bed and listen to you explain to the paramedics about your doctoring the poor man." Savannah sat down on the corner of the bed and crossed her arms.

Sadie recognized her daughter's stubborn stance. She'd been introduced to it when Savannah was less than a year old. The exact same stone-faced posture, every damned time.

"Let's not get testy with each other, honey girl, I'm concerned about the Senator. But I know he's okay.

"Kiss your velvet white ass? Oh my! Tell me, did you become so foul-mouthed because of me? Or did I become foul-mouthed because of you?"

"Get off my back for a minute, Mama."

"Savannah, darlin', please don't be so hard on me. You're my whole life, baby girl."

"Oh, here it comes, you and your damned guilt trips. Nip it in the bud, Mama! Nip it, nip it!"

Sadie laughed. "Sorry, Buttons, it's my best game—and it doesn't even work on you—never did."

Sadie heard Savannah let out a noise. She may have even mumbled something under her breath, but now wasn't the time for Sadie to start one of their wars. She'd let it go this time. There would be plenty of other opportunities for the two to spar. They'd been doing it for thirty years. Why stop when they had it honed to such a fine art?

"Mama, I'm calling an ambulance." Savannah walked over to a bedside table, picked up the phone and dialed 911.

"Child, are you trying to get me charged with attempted murder?"

"No more tricks, Mama. This is serious. You can't act like a doctor and decide when and how much medicine to give your husband."

Softly and barely audible, Sadie replied. "The hell I can't. He's my husband."

"Mama, the ambulance is on it's way. I'm going to check on Buddy again."

Sadie immediately turned to the mirror to check her hair, make-up and perfectly fitting jeans and top. As a last minute thought, she grabbed her diamond watch and added another diamond ring to complete her 'look'.

"Jesus, Mama, what's important here, Buddy's health, or how good you look?"

Sadie's left eyebrow spiked as she glared at her daughter. She stalked to her husband's bedside, checked his pulse then reached for the portable blood pressure machine. She placed the cuff on his arm as she continued to breathe fire, only breaking eye-contact with her daughter when she read the machine printout.

"His blood pressure is a little low, which is better than being a little high."

Sadie threw the blood pressure cuff on the floor, still not breaking eye contact with Savannah.

Sadie continued her prognosis. "His pulse is stronger than it was a few minutes ago and it is regular. Believe me, no husband of mine would die on *me*! He might actually leave me more money than he took from me. That would be something different, now wouldn't it?"

She paused, but only for a moment.

"And just to enable you to sit there and think of me as a selfish, raging bitch, my 'look' is a damned sight more important to me than anything about Buddy!"

Savannah stared at her mother. Surely she hadn't meant what she had just said.

"Mama, how many sleeping pills did you give him?"

"They weren't sleeping pills. They were *Xanax*. His nerve pills," Sadie answered softly and in a much calmer tone.

"You're going to have to tell the paramedics when they get here."

"No, I shan't. He's fine, and if he isn't, then I'll tell them what they need to know. We live in the South, sugah, if a woman kills her husband, everyone assumes he had it coming, and it would certainly be so in my case. Now, go put on some makeup and I'll answer the door when the ambulance gets here."

Their bickering was interrupted by the doorbell and the arrival of the paramedics.

Sadie rushed downstairs, calling back over her shoulder to Savannah. "Fix your makeup, honey, they're here."

"They're not here for a goddamned dinner party!" Savannah hissed back at her mother. But for some reason, followed her mother's instructions, took her makeup bag out of her purse on the way back to the bedroom. She'd just put on a little fresh concealer.

Sadie swung the door open and—attempting to drown out the vile language coming from Savannah at the top of the stairs—effused just a little too loudly to the paramedics, whom she had known most of their lives.

"Thank goodness you're here, darlings! Come on in, please. The Senator's really much better, he's upstairs."

Both paramedics hurriedly kissed Sadie on the cheek as they passed her, making their way to the Senator. Sadie took over the lead, explaining, step-by-step, the events of the evening. Almost as they had really happened. She left out the few details that incriminated her.

"He just seemed to be too deeply asleep. I feel foolish now. His blood pressure is 110 over 60. His pulse is strong and regular. I think he is fine now—he just got over-wrought. Savannah's with him." Sadie informed the paramedics with a smile as they walked into the bedroom where Buddy was.

"Hi, Savannah." Both young men greeted their friend.

"Hey, Jason. Hey, Jimmy." Savannah responded with a smile. She had learned from the best.

The paramedics started taking the vital signs of the Senator.

"Mama, is there anything you need to tell the boys? Did Buddy take any medicine that he shouldn't have? Or maybe more than he should have?"

"No, sugah, not so far as I know. He asked for his meds and I gave him his usual. I certainly hope he hadn't already taken any before then!"

Sadie and Savannah were staring at each other. Each with an eyebrow arched in defiance—not unlike dueling pistols.

As the women faced each other, Jimmy the paramedic came over. "Mrs. Montgomery, you're right. His blood pressure is okay, his pulse is strong and regular. When I checked his eyes, he pushed my hand away and turned over."

"He's fine, but I think we should take him on to the hospital. Dr. Rush would have our butts if he found out we had been called out here and hadn't brought him in to be seen. He'll probably want to run some tests just to be absolutely sure," Jason the paramedic suggested.

"Thank heavens, he's alright. Yes, I'm sure it's best to take him to the hospital. We must be very careful with his health."

God! She could have been an actress. She even impressed her own lying self.

A third paramedic suddenly appeared with a gurney, and the three young men began gently transferring the Senator from his bed onto the gurney as they continued chatting with Savannah. They then all headed downstairs to the ambulance.

"I have a fresh-baked pie. Can I get you boys a piece? I'll make some coffee." Sadie, being Southern, raised to accommodate, automatically offered food and drink when anyone was in her home. The paramedics shook their heads and smiled.

"Good Lord, what's wrong with me?" Sadie was flustered. That was totally inappropriate. But she was so out of her element. To paraphrase Enheduanna, "her honeyed tongue was tied with confusion." It was improper to flirt, to be a proper hostess—what the hell was she supposed to do? So she hushed.

"I'll just grab my bag and I'll be right along. I'll follow you in my car." Sadie informed the young men.

She then turned to Savannah.

"Savannah, darling, I can't thank you enough for running to your step-daddy's side. You know he loves you like his own.

"But, now you need to go on home to Beau and those babies. I just hate myself for calling and bothering you. I just lost my head, darlin'. I'll call you from the hospital tomorrow when I find out something."

The paramedics were calling goodbye. Sadie and Savannah turned to say goodbye, and to thank them.

Sadie was still pretending to be hurt. "I guess you're sorry I'm not going to get the electric chair. But you can still suggest they give me a lie detector test, if you don't think I've suffered enough."

"We'll see." Savannah kissed her mother on the cheek and whispered in her ear. "Your mascara's smeared, Mama, and you need more lipstick." She hugged Sadie and quickly headed for her car.

Sadie was all too familiar with her daughter's evil sense of humor. She had probably said that to drive her nuts! But now, of course, she'd have to go back and check it. She went to the mirror. Sadie had never met a mirror she didn't like. Everything was perfect. Sadie should have known. That child was intent on driving her crazy!

On the way home, Savannah felt a little guilty about hitting her mother below the belt. But she had it coming, with all that 'presentation' shit! Savannah couldn't help but smile, despite her guilt, at her own achievement of attacking Sadie's vanity.

She loved her mother, but the claws came out instinctively on sight. Sadie was a wild and funny woman and she never gave up. But please God, Savannah thought to herself, don't give me all of her eccentric qualities. My husband would divorce me and my children would run away from home…straight to Sadie. Lord help me!

Savannah turned into her driveway. Her husband was sitting on the porch waiting for her. As she drove in, he got up and walked toward the car. Savannah jumped out and closed the door.

"Hey, Baby! Any trouble with the kids?"

"No, they're fine. How's Buddy?"

"He's okay, I think. The ambulance took him to the hospital for observation and to run some tests, but they think he's fine. Jimmy and Jason were the paramedics on duty. They said 'hey'."

Beau could tell that Savannah was exhausted from the experience, but he also knew she couldn't stay away from her mother. And, he had more than a sneaking suspicion she enjoyed the drama Sadie created, almost as much as Sadie did.

"How's your mom?" Beau asked with slight hesitation. He feared Sadie, but from afar. To let her know his fear, would be suicide.

Savannah laughed. "Oh, hell, Baby, she's Mama. I apologize for my crazy mother. She says the most awful, outrageous things, then she's shocked that I didn't realize it was a joke. Joke my ass!"

Beau laughed and put his arm around his wife.

"I got a call from my mom earlier. Wanna hear about it?" Beau asked Savannah.

"Only if it will make me feel better about mine." Savannah answered.

"It'll keep." Beau grinned.

"You sorry shit." Savannah laughed back at him as they walked arm and arm into the house.

"Remember, Babe, if your mom wasn't so nuts, you wouldn't be the fascinating woman you are, and I wouldn't be so in love with you—not even mentioning those great genes she gave you that make you so damned sexy."

Savannah hugged her husband tighter. "You sweet thing!"

2

*A*fter Savannah left Sadie's driveway, heading home, the ambulance pulled away, driving slowly, headed for the hospital. No sirens, no flashing lights, no damned emergency.

"That son-of-a-bitchin' husband of mine. I ought to pull that ambulance over, get in the back and shoot the bastard. God! I wish I had a gun." Sadie was talking out loud to herself—and she continued. "I shouldn't be afraid of guns. I grew up with rifles all over the house. The only thing about them that scares me, is the friggin' noise. That is so stupid. Oh, yeah, and that jerking and slamming against your shoulder. It hurt for days. If I tried to shoot a pistol, it would most likely flail about and I'd take out several defenseless citizens. Okay, I'm never going to have a gun. But I want one."

Sadie was working through all this as she pulled out of her driveway and fell in behind the ambulance, annoyed they were driving so damned slow.

God, she was tired. Tired of being up-beat, high-energy for everyone, all of the time.

Tired of all the damned drama the Senator constantly created. Why the hell did she marry him? She didn't like him. She didn't like being around him. And she sure as hell didn't like taking care of him.

The Senator had to have an audience at all times to whom he could bloviate. Unfortunately, he was spending more and more time at home and Sadie was his primary audience.

Sadie always tried to smile at his dumb remarks—which were increasing in number and becoming more idiotic for the most part. She would make the appropriate response and nods of agreement, even when she thought his opinions were unoriginal and equal to an adolescent's opinion—only not as well thought out. It was becoming more difficult to maintain her composure and to control her anger. It's a good thing she didn't have a gun. She would have shot him a week after she married him.

Tonight, Sadie thought, had been the last straw. He was aggravated with everything on the evening news. He was railing on about it all at the top of his voice. Then he decided to stay up for another dose on the late news. He took this edition of the news report with even more anger. He was drinking and getting louder and angrier.

Savannah had been right. Of course Sadie had known the Senator had already taken his evening meds, but when he asked Sadie to bring him more, she did. Without hesitation. Then, when he decided he wanted another drink, she popped a couple more in his glass, for good measure.

Oh come on! Any woman in her right mind would have done the same damned thing, IF she was dumb enough not to have a gun!

Yes, she had taken a chance of doing him some serious damage. And she couldn't have cared any less.

Here, take these, you jerk! As Sadie best remembered, those were the exact words she was screaming in her head as she doled out his medicine. Wishing she could pocket a few for herself, but if she got him shut up, she wouldn't need them. See how that works?

In fact, if he hadn't shut up, she would have given him more pills!

She was so damned relieved when he fell asleep. But then, when he seemed so deeply asleep and she felt his pulse was weak, then, in a panic, she called Savannah.

Now, sadly, she realized what she should have done. She should have taken a nice long stroll outside in the garden, smoked a cigarette, and let the son-of-a-bitch die of the heart attack she was convinced he was having. Well, hindsight and all that. No matter, apparently he wasn't having a heart attack. Also, she didn't smoke. That whole dramatic scenario was screwed from the start.

So, back to reality and her usual missteps.

After her panic wore off, she realized calling Savannah had been a stupid mistake. She hated upsetting Savannah, and always regretted turning to her in desperation. But, that was always the first thing she did.

All Sadie had accomplished was to miss another night's sleep, cause Savannah to have to get out of her bed and leave her family, only to come hold Sadie's hand while scolding her at the same time. That part was hard to take.

Sadie was so damned mad at herself for that. Oh, well, she had it coming. She hated her desperate need for Savannah. It seemed Savannah had become the parent and Sadie the child. Having to explain her actions to her own daughter! When had that started?

She was beginning to feel sorry for herself and wished she had a tall glass of Walker's Deluxe Whiskey with a little 7-UP and a squeeze of fresh lemon juice. Just like Auntie Jaqleen had taught her to make. It was better when Auntie used to prepare it. She had a special touch. Auntie would make one, then Sadie would make it exactly the same way, but it would never be as good as Auntie's. And now, she had to manage on her own.

Oh damn it! Now she was fighting back tears. She missed Auntie Jaqleen so much. It would require a Walker's Deluxe and a couple of calm-me-down's to just relax, never mind sleep. Another lecture from Savannah would ensue if she found out just how much self-medication it required for only a couple of hours sleep.

Sadie almost bumped her head on the steering wheel. She had hit the brakes too hard when she realized she had run into the guard rail at the hospital parking lot.

"Well, shit!" She said aloud as she grabbed her purse and keys and slammed the car door. You're making a fool out of yourself, old woman!

My God! Sadie continued the internal dialog as she scrambled to get her purse and necessities together. I hope nobody saw that! There'll be talk all over town that I was drunk, or can't drive, I don't know which would be worse. Dammit, you are an old woman. You ought to keep your ass at home, bake pies and cakes, so you'll be ready for company, should anyone deem to come calling.

Get a grip! You have to be Sadie Montgomery when you walk into that hospital. Be who they expect you to be. You may not know who the hell you are, but everyone else seems to. They expect you to smile, gush over everyone and make them laugh.

And she would do it all, because her need for approval was still in the begging stage. Other people actually thought she had developed into that person. Sadie knew she hadn't developed at all. She was still that scared little girl from the foot of Crow Mountain.

Part of being Southern is the ability to deny reality. This comes in real handy. In fact, it's just a blessing, pure and simple, especially when one gets older. Practice it long enough and by damn, it works. Sadie had practiced it her entire life. It had saved her soul.

Sadie had chosen to display a sweet and graceful maturity, attempting to emulate her Auntie Jaqleen. Sadie actually did have a wisdom about her which she conveyed to anyone seeking her counsel. Sadly, it didn't work on her.

Sadie was gentle and kind. She had been born an old soul. Her childhood had made her feel old, burdened and battered. She fought this with laughter, but made little attempt to control her sharp, cynical wit; mostly because it provided that fabulous extra bonus of self-entertainment. She was even more entertained with the delightful quips she said silently to herself, forbidding herself to speak aloud the best and the funniest. They were a little too harsh for public consumption,

Sadie found herself at the hospital entrance. She managed to get herself together and followed the gurney into the emergency room. The nurse behind the desk came out to give Sadie a hug. This nurse was one of the biggest gossips in town. Every move Sadie made would be reported by Nurse Mattie. Big-mouthed bitch. Sadie reasoned that Mattie had probably been a colicky child.

"We've been waiting for you. The paramedics radioed ahead and we're all set up for the Senator. Now don't you worry. We'll take good care of him. He's going be fine." Nurse Mattie assured Sadie.

Oh, Shit! Thanks!

Sadie was glad when she saw that the nurse's expression hadn't changed. That meant she hadn't said that out loud.

The nurse was still talking. "We'll get him all settled in and comfortable. We'll re-take his vitals before we call Dr. Rush to see what tests he wants us to run." She looked at Sadie for a reaction.

Sadie nodded and smiled instead of saying, I don't give a damn what you do to him, I just want to go back home and go to sleep.

The nurse mistook her silence for worry.

"He'll be fine, dear." She said as she patted Sadie's shoulder.

"Yes, I know. He's much better. I'm afraid I over-reacted. I'm embarrassed to cause such an uproar. I think he's fine now, but isn't that the way it always is? As soon as you get to the doctor's office or the hospital…it all seems better. And you just feel like a fool. Like I do now." Sadie was half confessing, half putting on her act. For Sadie, it was difficult to distinguish the difference anymore.

"Now, don't feel that way. You did the right thing. You take such good care of the Senator." The nurse tried to put Sadie at ease. Good luck with that. As the nurse rambled on, Sadie was mentally counting out the pills she had given him, wondering how many more would have done the job.

Miraculously, she was properly responding to the nurse. "Oh, you're kind. Thank you, but I feel terrible. I called Savannah; woke her up and she rushed right over, leaving poor Beau with the babies. She's going to kill me! She's much too busy for me to be bothering her all the time." Sadie couldn't control her rambling mouth.

"There's no way on earth Savannah feels that way!" The nurse tried to comfort. "Now, come in here and sit in the waiting room. It's empty, so you can relax until they get the Senator settled in, then you can go into his room. I'm going to bring you some coffee...black?"

"No, please, sugar and cream." Sadie said. "Thank you, dear."

"Mrs. Montgomery, are you sure you're okay? You look so pale. Please don't worry. The Senator is fine. The paramedics haven't found one thing to concern them."

"Oh, thank you. You've no idea how hearing that makes me feel." Sadie was sick at her stomach.

"Good. Now I'll leave you here to relax until the Senator is settled in." The nurse left the waiting room.

Sadie sat down and reached for a magazine as she waited for the nurse to bring her coffee.

Good Lord! This is all I need. Sadie was getting the shakes. In a more civilized day, it would have been the vapors. But, alas! Those days were gone! She had to snap out of this. Sadie always had these anxiety attacks when she was overly tired. And she'd been overly tired for the last twenty-some-odd years. She dug her nails into the palms of her hands, then stood up and started pacing. Had she brought an extra bottle of her calm-me-downs? Just the thought of being without them made her shaky.

The nurse arrived with Sadie's coffee. Sadie gave her a smile. "You're a darling, thank you."

"Can I get you anything else, Mrs. Montgomery?"

You can get the hell out of my face for five freakin' minutes, you twit!

"No, you've done more than enough. I'll just wait 'til I hear from you about the Senator." Sadie was glad the right response came out. She gave herself kudos for still being on the top of her game even under these circumstances.

The nurse patted Sadie's hand and turned to go as Sadie poured on her sweetest smile watching the nurse return to her post. Nurse Mattie would call every one she knew to report Sadie's actions, what she was wearing and how she looked. Having been surrounded by people like Mattie all her life, had made Sadie obsess over her makeup, hair and wardrobe. And Sadie had looked different as a child. She'd been laughed at. She was pretty, but she had grown up poor, skinny and draped in her tall, voluptuous sister's hand-me-downs. As she grew, the laughter stopped but Sadie had become a woman with a mission. She was determined to develop her own style and substance. She would not be ridiculed again. Criticism was not a friend to Sadie.

During Sadie's childhood, she had been pretty, but her ill-fitting clothing had been much too large for her, apparently, making her a source of ridicule among her peers. Something of which Sadie forced herself to deny at the time. Or, at least, she had done an expert job of burying the ridicule. When she left home after graduating at seventeen, her mission to be admired and even envied, had begun.

Sadie put down the magazine. She sipped her coffee, waiting for someone to come and get her.

How many times and for how many people had she sat in this waiting room, or one just like it? Waiting to be told some news—good or bad. Many, many times in her fifty-five years. Her father, her Auntie, other special relatives and good friends.

God! You live this long, things happen. Shut up! Come back, woman! Remember—you're Sadie Montgomery. Think shallow.

Sadie pulled out her compact to touch up her make-up.

GAWD! Who the hell is that old woman with puffy eyes and sagging jowls?

Holy Shit! Prepare yourself before you pull out that weapon again! Remember, never look at the entire face at one time. She put the compact back in her purse and attempted to compose herself.

Come on, you look great for fifty-five. Fifty-five! Are you kidding me? What the hell?! How did that happen? How could this possibly be? Well, this just sucks out loud!

Never mind. It's happened. Make the best of it, and for God's sake, don't let anyone know how scared you are!

At that moment, a handsome young man entered the waiting room. He looked familiar. Sadie smiled at him. Then she noticed he had a little tape recorder and a notebook. Oh, Good Lord—the Press!

"Mrs. Montgomery? I'm Jim Wilson with the Gazette. I just learned Senator Montgomery has been brought to the hospital. I'm so sorry to bother you, but would you mind giving the paper a statement regarding his condition?"

Sadie immediately morphed into the Senator's wife, Sadie style. After all, Jim was charming, divorced, no children and loved his job. These were all aspects that put Sadie into flirt mode as well.

"Oh, Jim, of course I remember you. How nice to see a familiar face. Please sit here by me.

"First of all, I'm sure the Senator's fine, but they are going to run some tests. I expect to hear something any minute. Let's get you some coffee."

"No, no, Mrs. Montgomery. I know where it is. I'll go get it." The reporter was thrilled! He got up to fetch himself a cup of coffee. One thing the media could always depend on, he thought, the Senator's wife relished the lime light. She was a lovely woman, loved by all. Okay, loved by most, the reporter acknowledged to himself. He was just glad to be in her good graces right now.

When he returned with his coffee, he sat down beside Sadie. "I appreciate you're not throwing me out. Any other politician's wife would."

"No, Jim, I'd never do that. I realize you have a job to do. I don't consider you intrusive in fact, I find your presence comforting.

"However, I just remembered I was supposed to have called the Senator's aide and a couple of his staff members. I completely forgot. I'll be in so much trouble. I'm a lousy politician's wife." Sadie was fishing for as many compliments as she could get. That always made her feel better.

"I find you quite charming. In fact, all the members of the press admire you and appreciate your kindness."

"Then, will you let me make my phone call, Jim? And pretend you're not here? So when they arrive, I can plead ignorance. I do that well." She smiled at him, thanking him with her eyes for falling under her spell.

Jim smiled back at her and thanked her. He stepped out of the room to give her privacy to make the necessary phone calls.

After a few minutes, she motioned Jim back into the waiting room.

"I've covered my ass, so come back. Now, tell me about yourself. Talk to me. Distract me." Sadie commanded.

Jim and Sadie were deeply engrossed in conversation when the nurse came in to tell Sadie that the Senator was settled in his room and asking for her.

Jim asked Sadie if he could wait there, just until he was told something he could report.

"Only if you call me Sadie, and don't rat me out when his aide gets here. He or one of the Senator's staff should give you the official report. Sorry, I abandoned protocol altogether. I can assure you the Senator's fine—but let them tell you—it will make them feel so important."

Sadie and the reporter laughed. He touched her shoulder. "Thank you, Sadie. I won't rat you out. I enjoyed your company."

Sadie smiled and turned to follow the nurse down the hall to the Senator's room. *Oh, Lord have mercy! I'm flirting! My knees are a little weak. I was seriously flirting! God! I'm such a slut! Albeit an inactive one. Any chance the nurse hadn't noticed? Like I care what that twit thinks about me.*

Nonetheless, Sadie obediently followed the nurse into her husband's room.

The nurse was gushing on and on.

"Oh, the Senator's sleeping again. All his vitals are good. But I knew you would want to be in his room with him until they start the tests that Dr. Rush has ordered, in case he wakes up again. Dr. Rush will be here in about an hour and they'll get the tests started."

Sadie's mind answered again…*How wrong you are, sweetheart! I don't want to be in his room or anywhere near the bastard, and how dare you assume you know what I want!*

23

But, she was pretty sure her voice was saying, "Of course I want to be here with him. Thank you for being so considerate."

The Senator was sleeping peacefully. Sadie smiled at the nurse as she hurried back to her post. Then Sadie glared at the Senator.

"Sleep well, you inconsiderate bastard." She said, almost too loudly.

Sadie sat down in an uncomfortable chair next to the Senator's bed. She stared at him.

"I'm tired, Buddy. Why the hell can't I ever sleep and you sleep like a baby? You annoy the hell outta me. I think I'm going to have an affair. Maybe with that charming reporter." She had no concern that she was saying all this out loud.

She wondered how long it would take her to firm her ass so that she could have an affair. She had neglected her visits to the gym as of late.

"You don't care, do you? I could never catch up with your escapades, could I?" She asked her husband's restful face.

Oh, Lord have mercy. Why are all of Tennessee Williams' plays running through my mind at a frenetic pace? His plays were slow, lazy and with incredibly sexy, brilliant dialogue.

Sadie wanted to be one of those languid, sensual women from Tennessee Williams' mind. But, Mr. Williams would never have wasted his time writing about the likes of a sniveling twit like Sadie. Too bad she had never met him. She could have explained.

A knock on the door startled her back from her imaginary chat with Tennessee Williams over glasses of bourbon. It was the Senator's aide. Sadie greeted him and updated him on every detail of the Senator's non-existent crisis. Then, offhandedly, she mentioned that she thought she'd caught a glimpse of Jim Wilson from the Gazette, in the waiting room.

"You might want to go in there and assure him the Senator's wife is a fool and panicked when she discovered the Senator sleeping soundly and immediately called 911." Sadie instructed.

The aide laughed. "Better safe than sorry, Sadie. I wonder how Wilson heard about the Senator?"

"Well," Sadie said thoughtfully. "The paramedics radioed the hospital that they were bringing the Senator in. I'm guessing there are many people who monitor these calls. Surely a clever reporter would monitor all such calls, including police calls.

"Sorry I didn't call you before I left the house, David. I had other things on my mind." Sadie was effortlessly giving her excuses, covering her tracks. It came easy to her. But the Senator's aide was looking at Sadie a little strangely. He recognized that she sounded a little hard. It wasn't like her. He quickly dismissed it, though. Circumstances were not usual by any means.

"No harm done." David reassured. "I'm glad the Senator's okay. You have always taken very good care of him, Sadie."

Sadie looked at him like she was going to say something he didn't want to hear. The Senator's aide spoke first.

"I'll go appease the press. I'll check back with you later." He turned to go.

"You're a good friend, David. Thank you." Sadie smiled him out of the room. She was good at that.

Sadie sat back down. She started getting pissed off at the Senator again as soon as she saw his face. She instinctively continued her ranting.

"Lucky me. They have allowed me to stay in your room and watch you sleep. Hell, I can do that every night. God knows I can't sleep. In fact, I'm so tried I can hardly hold my head up."

Sadie closed her eyes and her mind wandered. God, a hospital can be so quiet at four o'clock in the morning. Makes you think sad, lonely thoughts. If it weren't so damned early, she'd call her best friend, Caroline, for comfort.

She decided to cheer herself up by thinking about her darling Savannah, Beau and those precious children. Little Roger Montgomery and Catherine Virginia. What joy they brought her. She was able to keep them with her more now that Savannah had finally allowed herself to go back to work. And she stayed so busy. Sadie missed Savannah's company, but how wonderful were those kids! Funny little Catie Vee. The very image of Savannah. And Roger Montgomery, that darling boy—just like his daddy—Perfect!

For all the pain in Sadie's life, her reward was this little family and Beau's extended family. Then there was Sadie's own sweet sister, her two brothers and their families. They all lived in San Diego. So, Sadie didn't see them often. The great tragedy of their lives was the loss of their beloved brother, the youngest, the sweetest, most vulnerable and fragile—as it turned out. Oh that unbearable sadness.

Sadie was jerked to the present by the nurse arriving to tell her they were going to take the Senator down to start the tests. Dr. Rush had called in a slew of them and he was on his way to the hospital.

Good grief! It's 7:30 a.m. How Sadie would love to crawl into a nice comfy bed and go to sleep. She should be able to do that—but oh, hell no. Instead, she told the nurse she would be down in just a minute. Sadie thought it best to take this opportunity to freshen up.

Her anger at her husband had subsided for the moment. At least he loved Savannah, Beau and the kids. Sadie would give him credit for that—not to anyone's face, however. And, she'd give him credit for little more!

Sadie came out of the ladies' room looking somewhat refreshed. She headed down to X-ray where they had taken Buddy. She visited with the technicians and nurses while the tests were being run. Dr. Rush arrived and assured her the Senator was fine, but there were a few more tests he wanted done. He told Sadie she didn't have to hang around, but she knew better. She knew how it would look if she left her husband's side. And she definitely knew what she would be facing when he called for her and she wasn't there to jump to his requests, whatever they may be.

"I just wanted to see your pretty face, Sadie. It cheers me up to have you close by," he would say, particularly after he had sent someone to find her, as though she were a child to be kept after. The anticipation of his beckoning her sent a chill up her spine. Thank God the staff had the courtesy to keep him sedated for the majority of their stay thus far.

When the inevitable happened and the Senator became more alert, Sadie tried to explain to her husband that she had to take bathroom breaks and just get up and move around occasionally. She accepted his flattery sweetly and waited for him to fall back to sleep. She looked around for a morphine button to push, but didn't see anything in her immediate reach. As much as she loved flattery, she'd rather have a good night's sleep.

Sadie spent most of the morning visiting an old friend she knew was a patient, wandering through the hospital's gift shop, chatting with the volunteers and running back to the Senator's side often. If it weren't for the presence of the Senator, Sadie would have enjoyed herself. She loved socializing, and being charming and witty to everyone kept her from thinking about her own predicament.

3

*A*s Savannah and Beau were getting their day started, Beau noticed his wife was more distracted than usual.

"Something you need to talk about, Babe?" He asked as he gently kissed her cheek. He knew she had to be worried about her mother and step-father.

"I have to spend at least two hours on a conference call, then I can take the kids to your parents. I guess I've got to go ahead and check in with Mama first." Savannah faded out as Beau watched her flit around the kitchen, thinking out loud. She turned around and dialed the phone, almost oblivious to what was going on around her.

Sadie had turned her cell phone off. Great. Savannah mumbled something under her breath. Beau recognized some of her favorite expletives, but that was about all he could understand of what she had just said. She dialed another number, and another. Savannah was finally able to learn the good news of her step-father's condition from one of the nurses at the hospital. She was just as relieved to hear that Buddy was okay as she was irritated that her mother hadn't bothered to call and let her know.

Beau offered to take the children by his parents' to give Savannah some extra time. She practically melted into his arms with relief.

When the kids were dressed and had their breakfast, Savannah called them to come and give her a hug and kiss before they left.

"Roger Montgomery! Catie Vee! Come give your mama some love before you go. You're going to spend the day with Pap and Swooze while I get some work done, then I'm going to see about Poppa Bud." Savannah couldn't help but laugh at the names her children had come up with for their grandparents. For the most part, the names had just evolved from their learning how to say names. Savannah was appalled when her mother concluded that her grandchildren call her Sadie like everyone else.

"Why don't you just have him call you Mrs. Montgomery, Mama!" Granted, Sadie could have chosen a more opportune time to discuss the name issue. It was possible it wouldn't have aggravated Savannah so much if she weren't going on her sixth hour of intense labor with Roger Montgomery, when Sadie insisted they make a decision.

"Let it go, Buttons. Shouldn't you be screaming and pushing? You've got ten more hours of this before you can catch up to my childbirth story. Concentrate on having a grotesque birthing account for your baby." Sadie's voice went into a whisper as she leaned down to her daughter's ear to tease her further. "They'll love hearing about it every year on their birthday." Savannah was more than familiar with this tradition.

"Shut up, Mama, or I'll have you thrown out of here. Can't you see I'm in a little discomfort here?"

"Well, isn't it just like you to bring the attention back to yourself." Sadie snapped.

Savannah started laughing, but as a new contraction began, her laughter turned into a scream not unlike that of a wild animal.

"Damn, Savannah! Show some decorum here. Try to act like a lady. You know how people talk."

Back in her kitchen, Savannah finished up her reminiscing. Why did everything have to be more difficult when it came to pleasing her mother? Savannah realized she had wandered off on her own little tangent. Where had all that come from? She asked herself rhetorically. She knew exactly where it all came from. She shook it off and held onto her kids.

Catherine Virginia and Roger Montgomery hugged and kissed Savannah long and hard. "Love you, Mama! Tell Sadie and Poppa Bud we love them. Give Sadie a kiss for me! When will you come and get us?" Their instructions and questions were plentiful as they talked over each other, each vying for one more kiss from Savannah.

"I will, I will. I love you, too. I'll come to get you this afternoon. Be good for Pap and Swooze. Mama loves you!"

She kissed Beau and thanked him for the help. The help of sustaining some degree of sanity—or at least excusing the lack of sanity she was displaying. She wasn't thanking him for caring for his own children, she didn't have to. She went back to her office to take care of her conference call. She hurried through it, anxious to get to the hospital, but not so much out of concern for Buddy. She had been assured he was fine. She knew she had gone too far with Sadie. She loved her—but that protective guard reared it's ugly head as soon as they were in the same room.

Finally, about noon, Savannah decided she'd had enough time to strengthen herself for the 'Mama encounter'. She drove to the hospital and found Buddy's room. He was sound asleep and Sadie was staring out the window, resting her head in her hand.

Savannah's heart lurched. Her mother looked so tired. But she had been fooled by this martyr syndrome before. Damn her! How am I supposed to do and say the right thing when I have no idea if she's afraid she could have lost Buddy, or if she's pissed because he's made it through? Savannah took a deep breath, and a pill, and turned around and walked out of the room before anyone knew she had been there. She needed to re-group.

"Hey, Savannah!" Shit! Damn it! Nurse Mattie! Savannah knew her from growing up and she was quite sure she'd been on Sadie's heels since she walked in the hospital last night. Savannah quickly hushed her and pulled her by the arm, away from the door. This was quite a bit more physical than Savannah was used to being, but she knew how Mattie could be and, more importantly, Savannah needed time for her medication to take effect before she saw her mother.

"Mattie," Savannah scolded. "Please, my step-father is sleeping and I think my mother is too, I can't tell. She claims she never sleeps but I think she may have some kind of secret power she's trying to hide from me." Savannah had gotten a bit off topic. But she had done so on purpose, she knew she had acted inappropriately with Mattie and she was trying her best to play it off. It was times like these that she wished she could be a little more like Sadie.

Apparently, Savannah didn't realize how closely the proverbial apple had landed by the tree.

"I'm sorry, Mattie. I'm just a tad on edge about all this. Is there something my step-daddy needs, or can I have some time with them before you guys come in and check him out?" Savannah asked.

"Of course." Mattie sensed Savannah's nervousness and was smiling like a Cheshire cat. Nurse Mattie was taking a little too much satisfaction in watching the pretty and popular rival from high school days, frazzled and without proper makeup. "You go on in, hon."

Savannah smiled and turned her back on the nurse, and opened the door to Buddy's room again. Sadie sensed Savannah's presence, or else she'd heard her in the hall giving the nurse what for. Sadie turned around, her face lit up and she smiled.

"Hey, baby girl. I was afraid to call the house and disrupt things. Buddy's fine, as you can see. He's sleeping like a baby. Four hours straight now. All the tests have been negative. See, I didn't kill him after all."

Savannah went to her mother and hugged her. "I'm sorry I acted so harshly last night, Mama. I just worry about you."

"You only seemed worried about the Senator. You were pissed at me. Remember?"

Savannah gave an eye roll. "Sorry, Mama. It was an extreme circumstance." Savannah was getting pissed all over again. She had almost let it go, but apparently that would have made things too easy for Sadie. It was a shame that only half the things that the mother and daughter thought, were said out loud to each other. If they could communicate better, they might not be so suspicious of each other's words.

"Who looks the worse for wear this morning, Buttons? Your mama or your step-daddy? I wish to hell I could sleep like that. All I did was enable him to get the attention he craves and a good, long nap."

"Mama, I'm sorry." Savannah had no idea how to deal with this situation.

"Oh, don't be. You were right."

Savannah looked at her mother. Surely she hadn't heard her correctly. She'd been right? Her mother had just acknowledged she'd been right? Savannah heard her mother's voice again as the shock of this admission wilted.

"I gave him another dose of his meds after he had already taken some. He was ranting and raving and I really wanted him to shut up and go to sleep. Well, I got my wish, but I really would like a nap myself. As usual, I cut off my nose to spite my face! Wish to God I had a gun!"

Savannah heard the exhaustion in her mother's voice.

"Mama, please go home and rest. I'll stay with Buddy."

"Yeah, that'll work. Buddy will raise hell if he wakes up and I'm not here. And how will it look if I go off and leave my poor, sick husband? How selfish of me to try to get some sleep! God! This town would tar and feather me."

Savannah saw it coming. "I can't win this one. Can I sit here and you try to get some sleep knowing I'm here?"

"No. Just tell me about Catherine Virginia and Roger Montgomery. Who has them?"

"Pap and Swooze. I'm sorry I was so hard on you." Savannah was tearing up watching the sadness and exhaustion she saw in her mother's face.

"Don't do that, Buttons. Everything is fine. The doctor can't find anything wrong with Buddy. I, on the other hand, find many things wrong with him, but I'll keep them to myself for the moment."

Sadie had turned mischievous to bring a smile to Savannah's face. It worked, as it usually did, much to Savannah's chagrin. Savannah not only smiled she began laughing, this led to Sadie falling in with her laughter. They were surprised they didn't wake up Buddy with their spurt of completely inappropriate laughter.

"You're a caution, Mama. But you really do need to get some rest."

"Can't do it, baby. But you can go on now that you know Buddy's okay. I'll stay 'til they dismiss him. That's my cross to bear for marrying the son-of-a-bitch. I'll take my punishment. I'm a big girl. Now, you run along, I'll call you and let you know what's going on."

"At least come down to the cafeteria and eat something," Savannah pleaded.

"Lord, honey, is it lunch time? Sure, I'll go down with you. I'm famished. Can't remember the last time I ate. Besides, I'm going to cover every last foot of this joint to make sure everyone sees me and can confirm my devotion to Buddy."

Savannah's jaw dropped as she turned to look at her mother. Seeing the devilish look on Sadie's face, she should have known. They burst into laughter, again.

Savannah and Sadie were in the hospital cafeteria, looking over the buffet food. They had criticized, complained and generally trash-talked every item of food on display.

As they sat down with their plates, Sadie said "I have in front of me a plate of grease."

Savannah stared at Sadie's plate. "Well, for someone who is so particular about their food, I see you have managed to get five slices of bacon on your plate."

"Oh, honey. Bacon. Well, that's nature's candy, isn't it? I don't eat bacon except maybe twice a year. I mean, nothing is going to compare with our good cooking at home. Like, for instance, the cornbread dressing and Sister Mary's blueberry lush pie. Then there's that wonderful peanut butter pie. You know, that damned thing was so hard to make, I've only made it that one time."

Savannah's eyes got huge. "Yeah, but it was so good, I can still conjure up the taste."

"Good!" Sadie declared. "Then I won't have to make it again."

"Of course the candied yams can never be left out," Savannah said, her mouth watering.

"You know how I am about color," Sadie interjected. "We have to include the broccoli nut casserole. I've made that every year since before you were born." Sadie marveled.

Savannah looked up from her plate. "What broccoli nut casserole?"

"The one I make every Thanksgiving."

"You've never made that. I've never heard of it, nor have I ever eaten it."

"Oh, for Christ's sake, Savannah. I got the recipe out of a newspaper. No. It was a magazine. It was from Emmy Lou Harris. It was back in the 60's or 70's. I love Emmy Lou Harris, so I wrote down the recipe and have been making it ever since. You love it." Sadie made her final statement.

"Mama, I don't eat nuts in my food. You know that."

"Well, you sure as hell do! You eat them sometimes when you don't even know you're eating them. But I always make the broccoli nut casserole and you always eat it."

Savannah was exasperated again. "I've never eaten broccoli nut casserole and you have never made it when I was in your house."

"For the love of God, can we just drop it, then? If it's so important to you that no pecan has ever accidentally gotten into your mouth, then we can assume you never ate any of those pecan pies I make." Sadie was looking at Savannah as though she had just dropped in from another planet.

Savannah returned the look. "Well, a pecan pie is different. Can we just stop this, before someone gets hurt? We should never have a discussion when we have kitchen utensils nearby."

"Well said! Sometimes I think we will never have a normal conversation like other people do. No matter what it is, it turns into a debate. I don't know how that happens. I hate confrontation and arguments."

"Yeah, but you hate being wrong even more," Savannah came back at Sadie.

"Who wants to be wrong? I don't think I'm competitive. Oh, but you're right. I sure as hell hate to be wrong. I guess that comes from always being wrong. Especially, as far as you are concerned. *Okay! Okay!* I quit. I took it too far. See what I mean? Now, let's just hush and eat."

They both got quiet. Then Sadie giggled; which, of course, set Savannah off. In seconds, they were hysterical with laughter. They couldn't stop. Everyone in the cafeteria was staring at them. A waitress came by to offer them more iced tea. They waved her away, unable to speak. In fact, realizing they were making a scene, insured this state of hysteria was going to last for awhile. They had always had this effect on each other. Sadie was thankful that, if nothing else, she'd been able to teach her daughter to see humor in everything. Even great tragedy; especially, tragedy.

Finally, they regained control enough to sip a little iced tea and nibble around on the food.

"Bacon is nature's candy? Where in the hell did you come up with that shit?" Savannah had started smiling, but suppressed the giggles bubbling just below the surface.

"Oh, nothing is original. I probably read it or heard it somewhere."

Savannah shook her head and started laughing again. "I don't think that's a common saying, Mama. I never hear stuff like that. Guess we run with different crowds."

"No shit!"

They started laughing again. This time, control arrived sooner.

But, Sadie just couldn't control her damned mouth. We all knew this was coming. The question is, why did it take so long for Sadie to start something?

"Sweetheart, why didn't you wear one of those new outfits you got last week? One of those and a little more make-up would add some color and keep you from looking so tired."

Savannah literally let her head fall onto the table. "Dammit, Mama!"

"Savannah! Good God! What's wrong with you? You could have cracked your skull wide open. You'd half kill yourself just for the dramatic display. I know crazy runs in our family, but sometimes, child, you flat-out take it to a gallop."

Savannah had had enough. "I'm going to leave now, while we can still pretend to love each other." Savannah got up from the table, exhausted from another round with Sadie.

"I love you, Buttons. Don't be mad."

They hugged and kissed and pretended the foregoing, ridiculous, Sadie-instigated, exchange had never transpired. It was the only thing they could do to make their dysfunctional mother/daughter relationship work. Pretend it never happened.

Savannah felt better after getting Sadie to eat, but she knew that was all Sadie was going to let her do, so she sucked it up and left the hospital.

Sadie was left to entertain Buddy. All the tests had been run and eventually he was declared fit to return home.

"That's wonderful!" Sadie asserted with great conviction. But to herself, she whimpered. Not my home! Please, can't you find another reason to keep him here? Just don't let him come to my home!

Instead, she bubbled over with fake enthusiasm as she packed up his belongings and he politicked his way into a wheelchair, through the halls and continued as the nurses got him settled into Sadie's car.

The drive home was boring as hell. The Senator droned on and on about how close he had come to dying.

"Oh hell, Buddy! All your tests were negative. You are fine. Besides, you couldn't have died on me, I wouldn't have anything to wear to the funeral. My red velvet jumpsuit's still at the cleaners."

Buddy laughed. "Oh, Pretty Lady, you keep me alive by keeping me laughing!"

Well, shit! Sadie found she had defeated her intentions once again.

By the time Sadie got the Senator home and settled in bed, it was 9:00 p.m. The doctor had suggested Buddy stay overnight in the hospital, but of course, the Senator wouldn't hear of it. If his tests were all good, why should he spend another night away from home?

Why indeed? Was Sadie's response as she had listened to her husband talk to the doctors, and anyone else that would listen. Perhaps for my sake, you inconsiderate bastard! Oh, just let it go. My damned luck. Sadie had continued with her silent rampage, the whole time with a smile on her face. I'd just have to stay with him anyway!

Maybe I could check myself into the hospital! She began to ponder the different symptoms she could divulge to get herself a nice, private hospital room all to herself. But the bastard would just stay with me every minute! And, he'd expect me to entertain him or listen to him and respond enthusiastically. I can't win. I'll just take the jackass home. Sadie snarled, caught herself, and lovingly escorted the Senator out of the hospital.

Back at home, Sadie gave Buddy his night meds and took her own. To her relief, he went to sleep around ten. She didn't bother to determine if his sleep was normal, deep, coma-like, or even—dead. She was no longer interested. Besides, she knew how her luck ran. Cold.

Sadie went downstairs to the kitchen. She immediately felt relaxed. She loved her kitchen, especially without Buddy in it.

She prepared herself her Walker's Deluxe special, toasted the sweet memory of Auntie Jaqleen, and settled into a chair at her little glass table.

She tried to feel relief that Buddy was well and home—and she hadn't been arrested for attempted murder. She needed to look at the bright side.

But, damn it! She had been angry with him at least fourteen of the seventeen years they had been married. She couldn't really remember why she had married him in the first place. Or any of the others, for that matter.

Oh, at the time, they all had perfectly good reasons why it was essential that she marry them, but her heart had never been in any of them. She had spent the night before each marriage, crying herself to sleep. She had a real distaste at the thought of each of them. She never really forgave. She just became indifferent.

At this remembrance, Sadie finished off her drink and went into the living room, grabbed her favorite old quilt, and curled up on the sofa. She couldn't abide the thoughts which were coming fast and strong in the silence. She found a boring documentary on television and finally drifted off to sleep.

Sadie was awakened the next morning at 5:30 a.m. to Buddy's yelling.

"Sadie! Where are you, Sadie? When did you get up? Sadie? Sadie!"

Sadie quietly let out a string of her favorite curse words, got up and slowly walked upstairs to the bedroom. Never responding to his yelling until she reached his door.

"What's wrong, Buddy? Why are you yelling? Are you alright? Have you had a relapse?" Her voice was low and hard.

"I'm okay." Buddy was completely calm, now. "I just expected you to be here in bed. It upset me when you weren't here. Where were you? When did you get up?"

"I was in the kitchen, Buddy. What do you want and why couldn't you get out of bed and find me instead of yelling at the top of your voice?"

"Hell, Sadie. I expected you to be here. I always want you here. I get upset when you're not here." The Senator was trying to act pitiful.

Sadie wasn't buying it.

"How the hell can I be with you every minute and still start the morning coffee and do all my other usual chores?"

"Oh, is the coffee ready?"

Sadie would have thrown her body on the floor and unleashed an Oscar-winning temper tantrum if she thought it would help. But, she knew full well, she could do just that and, until she was done, Buddy would wait patiently. As soon as she was finished with her fantasy, award-winning fit, he would scold her like a six-year-old child; then, he'd remind her about his coffee.

The Senator was slowly getting out of bed—watching Sadie leave—expecting her to come back and get his robe for him. But, she kept walking. The lady was not in the mood to cater to him this morning.

She had the coffee started when her husband wandered in. "Where's the paper?" He asked in an annoying voice. He looked at his plate in disbelief that there was no newspaper beside it. "Isn't it here yet?"

That's it! Sadie started slamming pots and pans around in the kitchen simply to release her anger. She was just picking things up, knowing she had no intention of using it, and throwing it back down. She was exhibiting extreme self-control by not throwing them at Buddy. Somehow, this little tantrum failed to register with Buddy, which is why he went on about his own needs, oblivious to the fact that he was being such a jackass.

Sadie stopped everything and turned to him, hands on her hips. "I'll just bet that sucker's still on the porch." Sadie answered. "Do we need to hire someone to live-in, so one can be at your side twenty-four hours a day? And you'll need yet another to fetch and carry for you! I just can't seem to do all of that, Buddy! But have you even noticed that I sure as hell try? I'll trot my ass out front right now and get you that newspaper. God forbid you should exert yourself in any way and do just one fucking thing on your own!"

Sadie strode briskly to the front door to retrieve the newspaper from the porch. Damn! She was so angry with that demanding, inconsiderate bastard, that she was having difficulty getting her breath. She slammed the door behind her and slapped the paper down in front of him.

"I'll bring your coffee to you as soon as it's ready."

"Now, Sweetheart, don't get mad. I just got out of the hospital, I'd think you would be a little more understanding." Still no, 'thank you.' It wasn't that Sadie expected one, she'd been with him long enough to know that wasn't coming. Actually, she was surprised he wasn't asking why she hadn't provided his coffee before going to get the newspaper. She'd said she'd been down here making it.

"Yes, Buddy, you just got out of the hospital. You were only in the hospital because I'm an idiot!" Her voice was rising.

"I'm so stupid, I thought something was wrong. You were sleeping so soundly! I don't sleep, so I found this frightening!"

Now she was yelling.

"I'm a freakin' idiot to worry about you! You don't appreciate me, yet I'm working myself into an early grave having to put up with your shit, day in and day out, and trying to please you so you won't have one of your mad fits! But you have them anyway. Nothing I do matters. You're just a selfish bastard. I'm done trying to please your hateful ass.

"Get your own damned coffee! I'm going to the sun room. Stay the hell away from that area of the house. If I don't get some sleep and rest, I swear to God, I'll kill somebody. Guess who?

"You know, if I'd shot you when I met you, I'd be out of jail by now!" She arrived at the proper finish to her tirade. Fearing she was going to pass out, Sadie whirled around and practically ran to the sun room. She closed and locked the door behind her.

She lay down on the day bed and tried to take deep breaths and relax. She knew Buddy wouldn't come near the room. 'Praise God From Whom all Blessings Flow' for that little favor.

She realized she hadn't spoken with Savannah since the day before. She reached for the phone and dialed Savannah's number.

Still feeling pissed off at the world and a little hurt by Savannah's scolding, first regarding the whole 'drugging Buddy' incident, then, at the hospital. Savannah had been quite upset that Sadie had turned off her phone and she had to learn about Buddy's condition from a random nurse at the hospital. Then, there was the whole cafeteria misunderstanding, Sadie found she still had a touch of irritability toward her daughter left in her.

When Savannah answered, Sadie said softly, "Good morning, darlin'. First of all, Buddy's fine and at home safe and sound, but you were right. They found an excessive amount of Xanax and alcohol in Buddy's system and he told them he didn't remember taking it, so, I'm calling you from jail."

"Oh! Dear God, Mama! I'll be right there!"

Before Savannah slammed the phone down, she heard her mother's voice again.

"Aww, I'm just funnin' with you, sugah. We're settled back at the house. Buddy's fine. He's having coffee and reading his paper."

"What a bitch! Mama, you could have given me a heart attack! Do you think that's funny?" Savannah, in spite of it all, was smiling slightly, now. It actually was funny.

"No, giving you a heart attack would not be funny. But you were trying to have me put under suspicion of attempted murder. Glad you changed your mind." Sadie had done her job of insuring her daughter knew she had not forgotten her lapse in devotion the night of Buddy's unfortunate hospitalization.

"Jesus. Mama, you're crazy. And that was a horrible thing to do to me!" Funny, but horrible, Savannah confessed silently.

"Sorry, baby. I've had a lousy couple of days and now I'm regretting that I didn't kill Buddy. But, my luck has never been any good."

Savannah was on the other end of the phone sitting in a chair with her head between her legs, trying to breathe again. Her mother was crazy! But, she couldn't stay mad at her. That was the part that drove Savannah the craziest. She had actually caught her breath and was laughing at her mother's completely inappropriate sense of humor when she heard her voice again, she lifted her head. But she still needed the assistance of her hand to hold herself up.

"I just called to check in," her mother explained. "I'm going to try to get some sleep now. I'm sorry, baby girl. I just had to wind down after realizing Buddy was still alive and had come home with me. It was such a disappointment. But, I shouldn't have taken it out on you and upset you."

"Mama, I never know when you're serious. But, that's what makes you Mama. I'll laugh my ass off later, okay? Thanks for calling. Mama, are you alright? Really?"

"Of course," Sadie responded tiredly. "Take care of my babies. We'll talk later on, honey. You have a good day."

"Get some rest, Mama. I love you."

"I love you too, Buttons. Peace out." And Sadie was gone.

After she hung up, Sadie remembered she hadn't spoken with her best friend, Caroline. She needed to call her before this was on the news. Sadie was dialing Caroline's number without thinking.

Sadie filled Caroline in on the details, then they chatted for a short while. Caroline, as usual, wanted to do something to help.

"Come over and kill this son-of-a-bitch. That would help me!"

"Would if I could," was Caroline's caring response.

"It's not the thought that counts, missy!"

They hung up, with Sadie promising to call if she could think of anything she needed.

4

*O*n the sun porch, settled in her favorite daybed, Sadie rolled over and closed her eyes. Her mind drifted to the past as it always did when she was still and quiet.

She remembered the day Savannah was born. That was the day Sadie found her calling. Her reason for living.

Of course, Sadie had chosen the world's sorriest bastard to marry and impregnate her. And that was the extent of his fatherhood. Lord, I hope he's dying a slow, painful death somewhere! Don't dwell, Sadie! She told herself, fast forward.

Sadie and Savannah had a symbiotic relationship that continued after the umbilical cord had been severed.

They had great fun and loving times together. Sadie spoiled Savannah as much as possible. The bad times always came when Sadie would re-marry, thinking she was improving Savannah's life. How stupid could one woman be?

Sadie proceeded to show everyone, however unintended.

Sadie had never wanted to be married, so she never imagined a wedding. Never dreamed of a beautiful wedding gown or any of the accoutrements. Such an odd thing for a Southern girl.

Good thing she never wanted a proper wedding, she sure as hell never had one. Never had a bridal shower, come to think of it. The absence of these very important milestones should have probably made her weepy, but, nope. Not feelin' it.

Each marriage had made things worse. She knew she was getting less than she deserved. On the other hand, it had been ingrained into her entire being throughout her childhood, that she would amount to nothing, deserved nothing and could accomplish nothing. She had tried to overcome this indoctrination. Some things just couldn't be unlearned.

Sadie back-pedaled like crazy to get out of these marriages. Then would try to re-coup what she had lost—financially, emotionally and every other way.

Each man just happened to need the exact amount of money Sadie had in her savings. They needed it for taxes or something equally as pressing.

Dear little Savannah trudged through it all, bravely, loving and supporting Sadie. And trying to live her life while Sadie continued to ruin her own.

Caroline had been around for most of this as well. Sadie's closest friend of twenty-five years, Caroline was always a source of support and great fun. Actually, Caroline only supported Sadie because of their strong friendship. She would question Sadie and she would try to talk sense to Sadie. But in the end, approve or disapprove, Caroline was there. True Southern loyalty.

This loyalty was a great and unexpected gift. Caroline kept all of Sadie's secrets. Can you imagine? Sadie had trouble keeping her own secrets.

Sadie marveled at Caroline's high standards and lack of critical judgment of Sadie's stupidity and idiotic choices. Sadie had a lot of superficial friends, but Caroline was the real thing.

Caroline was always up for a good time. Her daughter, Lucy, was the same age as Savannah, so they had outings for the benefit of the girls when they were young, but the moms managed to have fun also. Lucy and Savannah had dance lessons, horseback riding lessons, ice skating lessons— whatever they wanted. The girls remained friends, as did Sadie and Caroline.

Caroline had a good, solid marriage. How she and Sadie stayed so close was nothing short of miraculous.

Caroline delighted in the steamy or funny details of each new "relationship." They had worked together, therefore Caroline was treated with daily reports on the previous evening's drama.

There were more issues to keep these women apart. Caroline didn't swear, had never smoked, but she would drink a little. Sadie was always in a bad marriage, trying to get out and trying even harder to avoid the next one.

Success evaded her at every turn.

Sadie was working in a political campaign again. She and Caroline often did this. Sadie had become interested in politics and volunteered in campaigns when she felt strongly about the candidate. She threw a lot of time and energy into the campaigns, believing she could get the right person elected who would make the world better for Savannah.

Caroline worked in campaigns when she believed strongly. Somehow, the campaign didn't become her entire life. Sadie, on the other hand, would encounter a huge variety of people and her social life would envelope her, almost against her will.

Work was a necessity, but working for a good candidate, she felt was an obligation.

It was at one of the many political social events Sadie attended that she met the Senator. He was dynamic, handsome and charming. The usual phony politician. He was just so damned good at it.

He was smitten with Sadie at their first encounter.

Although Sadie was married at the time she first met the Senator, she was running a hundred miles an hour with her hair on fire, trying to get out of the marriage.

In addition to Caroline, Sadie's Auntie Jaqleen had been her best friend and confidante. They both saw that, yet again, Sadie was in a destructive marriage. They helped Sadie build the strength to finally leave. Alas! Free of another one!

Now that Sadie was free, she absolutely was not interested in another. She just wanted fun, unencumbered affairs and nothing to do with the Senator. Charming as he was, she hated being married and was always happy to get each damned man out of her house.

Well...it never worked that way. The man always got the house and Sadie and Savannah had to move into another apartment. Leaving half of their furniture. And start all over again.

This was because, as each husband would carefully explain to her, his salary was at least three times hers. Each husband had enjoyed explaining this at frequent intervals throughout the relationships. She would have to leave. She couldn't afford the mortgage, or the utilities for that matter. Even so, for Sadie, it was worth the loss to be rid of the latest jerk.

Despite urging from family and some friends, Sadie was in no mood to take on another one. So, while Sadie was happily enjoying her freedom, the Senator patiently waited.

He showered Savannah with attention, knowing how important this was to Sadie.

Sadie enjoyed the attention she received from being photographed on the Senator's arm at political events. He was a very popular Senator, and Sadie, with her good looks, constant sense of humor and open friendliness, was a great asset to him. He was determined not to lose that.

Sadie continued to have relationships with other, younger men. These relationships were far more enjoyable.

Caroline saw through the Senator immediately. She would strongly agree with Sadie when they discussed his shortcomings. But she stopped there. She wouldn't point out anything Sadie didn't mention.

The Senator tried to cultivate Caroline's friendship. She put up a good front, but she was exasperated with this gas bag and with Sadie, for once again allowing a man to manipulate her. But, as usual, after a couple of years, the Senator wore Sadie down.

Sadie had two steamy affairs during her pre-marital relationship with Buddy. She had successfully hidden them from him. She knew from these affairs that Buddy was not who she was looking for. But, as was her pattern, Sadie succumbed to his pleadings and promises. He also kept reminding her that she was on the down side of thirty. Now Sadie was scared.

Auntie Jaqleen finally acquiesced, saying, "Well, maybe this one could work. I want to see you taken care of."

Caroline just shrugged her shoulders and said, "I want you to be happy. I hope it works."

Sadie's response, "Jeeze, curb your enthusiasm. Can't I at least sport this gaudy little rock around, in my own ostentatious way, before I must once again admit I hate being in captivity?"

Sadie, Caroline and Jaqleen all became disillusioned not too far into the marriage. Sadie suspected her husband was having a little fling with a campaign worker. Auntie Jaqleen was certain of it, as she had witnessed a private rendezvous.

But, Sadie decided she would try staying in this marriage a while longer, and, of course, Jaqleen and Caroline stood by her.

So, Sadie rode out that episode, but not in silence. She used the Senator as she felt he was using her.

Then, just to be absolutely positive things were evened out, she had her own fling with a member of his staff. The revenge was so much more personal that way.

And so the games began.

Sadie and Buddy the Senator would stay together, but it would be tumultuous to say the least. Their relationship became a wicked game of opposition and revenge. If Buddy said *yes*, then Sadie said *no*. If Buddy stayed out all night, Sadie threw out his clothes. If Sadie threw out his clothes, Buddy cut off a credit card.

It was relatively harmless in the beginning.

5

*B*uddy, Sadie and Savannah settled into a lovely home. Buddy and Savannah got along fine. He had no children of his own, and he thought Savannah was a great kid. He was a little more permissive than Sadie. But he also took great pride in Savannah and attended her school functions right along with Sadie.

Buddy was proud of Savannah and her popularity. He was almost as proud of her academic accomplishments as Sadie.

Savannah was always on the go with her friends.

There would be some tension between Buddy and Sadie when Sadie would say 'no' to outings on a school night. Right in front of Savannah, Buddy would say, "Oh, let her go. She's young, let her have a good time." Sadie would have to give in or look like a royal bitch. Savannah accused her of that often enough anyway.

Sadie tried to keep the unpleasantries of her new marriage hidden from Savannah. She'd find out later, regarding what a miserable failure Sadie had been at this one, as well.

The marriage between Sadie and Buddy was anything but perfect, or even functional, if we're going to be honest. She left him once and went so far as to retain an attorney to file for divorce. The Senator begged, pleaded and did his usual dog and pony show. It just seemed easier for Sadie to stay. She wasn't up to losing another house and more furniture.

Three days after she made the decision to stay, Buddy stayed out until 2:30 in the morning. He called her to explain that he was with his staff, aides and some other politicians working on a planned push to get a bill through the Senate the next day. He told Sadie they were still at the Capitol in Buddy's office.

Of course, Sadie knew he was lying. She heard background laughter, women and men talking and music. Not really a conducive environment for deep political contemplation.

"You lying bastard! You're in a bar with women and you're drunk." She screamed at him.

Buddy was having difficulty forming his words. His speech was so slurred she had to make him repeat everything three or four times.

Sadie began yelling at him again. "You're drunk, you idiot! So just keep your ass right where it is! *Do not come home!*"

Buddy was indignant. Even denied having one drink. The man was a pathological liar.

Finally, Sadie had had enough. In her calmest voice she told her husband, "I'm hanging up. If you're not drunk, considering the way you're slurring your words, you've had a small stroke. So you'd better have one of your trusty 'aides' haul your sorry ass to the hospital."

She slammed the receiver down and went to bed. The only way he could redeem himself, as far as Sadie was concerned, was to get arrested for drunk driving or to have a wreck and kill himself.

He did neither. As usual, he rolled in after a couple of hours and parked half in the yard and half in the street. When he stumbled into the bedroom, Sadie greeted him with a resounding, "*Go to hell!*" She then stormed from the room and locked herself in a bedroom downstairs.

The most incredible thing about these ordeals, was the Senator would get up at six o'clock the next morning, shower, have his coffee and act as though nothing had happened. And looking none the worse for wear, he'd then saunter off to work.

After one of these late night screaming sessions, Sadie's heart would sink when Savannah would glide into the kitchen just as Buddy was driving away.

"Nice going, Mama."

Sadie would immediately start trying to explain what had transpired and why she didn't throw Buddy out. She would usually just shrug and say, "Sorry, kid. Life's hard. I don't handle it well." Savannah would roll her eyes and say nothing. But to Sadie, she knew "You're an idiot!" had to be running through Savannah's mind.

Savannah was the one person from whom Sadie longed for acceptance. Sadie desperately wanted Savannah's respect. Sadie felt absolutely sick at her stomach every time Savannah was privy to an account of her dysfunctional marriage.

Buddy would usually try to drive Sadie to her job. Want to have lunch with her when he could, and pick her up in the evenings. This would have been a convenience if there wasn't a running argument from the time they entered the car until she could scramble out.

Sadie complained about the little things along with everything else to Caroline. They had lost Auntie Jacqleen by the time things got this bad. Sadie missed her terribly. Auntie would have my hide if she knew the shit I was putting up with—and dishing out for that matter. Sadie had to admit, Jacqleen had always been her appropriate Southern lady conscious.

Caroline listened and tried to be supportive, but sometimes even Caroline would ask, "How much more of this are you going to tolerate?"

The end was getting closer when Sadie began to suspect Buddy was having an affair with his best friend's wife. At least she was the object of his latest infatuation. To do this to his best friend was, oddly enough, much more offensive to Sadie. Not only was Johnny a truly good guy, he trusted everyone, and really loved Buddy.

Sadie's suspicions about this affair began when Buddy started talking about Johnny's wife constantly. When he was infatuated with someone, he couldn't shut up about her. This time it was Sally Blevins. Poor Johnny's wife. Poor Johnny!

Johnny was short, heavy-set, not so attractive. Just sweet...and, as one would suspect, he was rich. Very rich. Johnny was the president of a bank. He sat on the board of three local non-profit organizations. He was highly respected in the community. And all this was what attracted Sally.

Sally was a piece of work. She imagined herself an elegant artiste. She also thought she could paint and she fancied herself a poet.

Oh, please! Sadie was of the opinion, as was most of their social circle, that Sally's painting would be best kept to the confines of her barn, which she so eccentrically referred to as her 'studio'.

Physically, Sally was a tad on the mousey side, same with her personality. Sally tried to compensate by buying outrageously expensive clothes, but unfortunately, she couldn't pull them off—except when it came to doing so for Sadie's husband, apparently.

Sally clamored to be on the A-List. She entertained extravagantly. She made sure her guests were the most influential and elite of the community. But most were bored with her, and her attempts to impress failed to win them over. For the most part, Sally was a bit of a pathetic joke.

But, please be assured that what was said about her among these most influential and elite citizens, was all meant in the best Christian way. "Bless her heart" they were often heard saying.

Continuing on, when it came to Buddy, as Sadie was far too familiar, he talked about the object of his obsession endlessly. He drank so much, he didn't realize he was rambling on and on about his best friend's wife to his own wife.

When Buddy stayed home and got drunk, Sadie was glad Savannah's room was so far away, or even better, Savannah was out for the evening. When she came in, Sadie and Buddy would stop arguing long enough to kiss Savannah and chat with her as long as she would tolerate them. Then she would kiss them good night and head for her room and the phone.

One night, Buddy came in late, drunk, and with yet another ridiculous story about where he had been and with whom. Sadie refused to ride to work with him the next day. After he left, she called her office and told them she was feeling ill and would be in around noon.

Sadie proceeded to go through the jacket Buddy had worn the night before. Good God! He was so predictable and possibly the dumbest bastard who ever drew breath.

There was a book of matches from the restaurant/bar where he had been the night before. Isn't there always? The name and phone number for Sally were on the matchbook flap. Isn't there always? Well, not Sally, let's hope, but a name, nonetheless.

"What an unoriginal prick," Sadie said aloud, as she was sitting on her bedroom floor with her husband's jacket contents strewn around her. As she continued her search, things only got better.

There was a napkin from the restaurant. Drawn on it was directions to Sally and Johnny's home. Sadie had been there, so had Buddy—apparently more times than Sadie. The map was just proof Buddy was smart enough to know he was too drunk to find his way.

The next thing Sadie saw on the napkin would bring a tear to the eye of most men's wives. Sadie actually laughed out loud at the immaturity and stupidity she had grown so very used to. Buddy had drawn a heart where the house was located. He was a romantic son-of-a-bitch, Sadie joked to herself.

Sadie looked at the phone and cocked her head. She slowly got up and walked over to it. She called Buddy at work. His receptionist answered and, in the sweetest voice Sadie could fake, she requested her husband be pulled from his meeting for just a quick second. Buddy didn't take long to answer Sadie's request.

"You sorry, worthless bastard!" Sadie got right to the point. She really had intended to take only a moment of his time. It was more than she wanted.

"Your best friend's wife?"

Sadie slammed the receiver down. She called Johnny next, and asked him if he would have lunch with her. He, of course, was most anxious to do so.

Sadie wasn't exactly sure what her intentions were. But that had never stopped her from taking action prior to knowing what she was going to end up doing.

They had barely started lunch when Johnny asked Sadie if she realized Buddy and Sally were having an affair. Sadie was a little surprised by Johnny's bluntness, but as an expert in these matters of underhandedness, she never let on that she was taken aback by his accusation. She admitted she had suspicions, but that was only because Buddy had been talking about her so much lately.

Johnny told Sadie he was filing for divorce and Buddy was going to be subpoenaed and named as the other party in an alienation of affection suit. No longer viable in this State, but destructive to reputations. Sadie should have been hurt, insulted...oh, so many feelings other than the ones she had.

She found it outrageously funny. She pointed out to Buddy later that night, how overtly tacky he was, and that this was going to make all the newspapers. Sadie would be publicly humiliated. He was sure as hell going to pay for this one!

Sadie laid this next one on him with great jubilation.

"Buddy, I quit my job today. I can't trust you and I can't stay up all night waiting for you to come in drunk, then fight with you till the sun comes up, then get ready and go to work without any sleep.

"Can't do it, pal. Guess you're going to have to take care of this household on your own, since you can't behave your sorry self. Seems I can't tend to my wifely duties and hold down a full-time job. I think I also need that extra time to keep an eye on you!"

Buddy was speechless at first. Then, he just shrugged his shoulders and said "You don't have to work if you don't want to. And I'm not doing anything, so I don't know why you think I have to be watched."

"Oh, please! Savannah is more trustworthy and responsible that you are and she is wild as a March Hare."

Buddy was taken to court regarding his friend's divorce. But it was done quietly. Nothing appeared in the papers or on the television news. The Senator still had friends in very high places.

Sadie was a tad disappointed, but not terribly surprised that he wasn't more publicly disgraced. However, there was gossip aplenty. And Sadie took huge advantage of this. The Senator was extremely uncomfortable. He knew this would not have been enough punishment for Sadie's taste. Therefore, her plans for his punishment for this current indiscretion were still in the formative stage. He could only wait and imagine her retaliation.

One discussion with Caroline was very productive. Caroline, who would never allow a piece of costume jewelry to touch her body, suggested Sadie deserved a pair of ostentatious diamond earrings. Sadie was delighted with this suggestion and within hours, she was strutting around with her three carat diamond stud earrings. She liked them so much, she demanded Savannah have an identical pair.

This had made her feel much better, but, she always insisted retaliation be in the form of an eye for an eye. A cocktail party some days later, provided Sadie with some intriguing information. A woman with whom she had worked, was a bit in her cups and told Sadie of a young man, as in twenty years younger than Sadie, whom she knew and had just found out, had had a crush on Sadie for some time. This woman told Sadie she had overheard him telling a couple of men how sexy, smart, charming, and just plain gorgeous he thought Sadie was.

Sadie tried not to act too interested, but she made sure she got the young man's name and where he worked.

Within a couple of days, she managed to be at a gathering he was sure to attend. It took only minutes for her to look up and catch him staring at her. She smiled and walked over to him. Sadie didn't care that the Senator would hear about this. Quite the opposite, actually.

The much needed, enjoyed and appreciated affair went on for a couple of years. They had quite a grand frolic. They laughed all the time. He was very appreciative of her, and indeed, she was equally appreciative of him.

Sadie and her young lover actually had long conversations about things they found intriguing. They were truly interested in each other. No competition. No criticism. Everything about the relationship was positive and productive for both. Certainly Sadie's life was enriched by his presence in it.

But, it was doomed from the start. Primarily because Sadie reminded herself every day, he was half her age. It was a satisfying excuse for Sadie when the end did arrive.

Happily, the bond remained. They would always be able to greet each other with smiles, be pleased to see each other, and remember their sweet secrets.

Once during the lengthy affair, the Senator dared accuse Sadie of this infidelity. Sadie went into a screaming rage. She brought up everything he had ever done, and some things he wasn't sure whether he'd done or not!

She told him she would never forgive him for his disloyalty and disrespect. And, how dare he attempt to bring her down to his level?

The woman did possess a talent for turning the tables.

"If you dare accuse me of anything again, I'll sleep with one of your aides, or a staff member, or maybe another Senator…or how about a Governor?"

Her husband was terrified. Especially when Sadie announced that everyone was talking and they were expecting Sadie to inflict her revenge.

"I have a decision to make." She proclaimed. "And it all depends on how you act from here on out."

"I'm so sorry!" her husband said with a hangdog attitude.

"You don't know what sorry is, but I'm about to demonstrate for you." Sadie threatened. "You have humiliated me far too many times. I can hardly hold my head up in public. I'm terrified to go into any store, afraid someone will be there that you're sleeping with.

"Do you know what it feels like to be that nervous about what your spouse is doing? And how much everyone knows? I know everyone knows about your sleeping around. The difference is, everyone in town knows with whom and for how long. You don't even have sense enough to hide what you're doing, you stupid waste of life! I tend to blame that on your being drunk, but maybe, it's just you. It doesn't even matter to me any more. Either you are a person without morals or you are a drunk who has destroyed most of his brain cells!"

Buddy was so worried he started apologizing for things Sadie hadn't yet found out about. She just shook her head in amazement.

Sadie spent every night for the next six weeks in her favorite downstairs bedroom off the sun room. One morning she went in to the kitchen to find a beautiful diamond watch in a fancy box beside her coffee cup. Sadie was happy to have the watch, but the end of her revenge was not in sight.

It might lapse from time-to-time, but was always just below the surface. For now, Buddy had subdued Sadie. They would resume their regular routine.

Sadie continued to reminisce about the many things regarding the Senator that angered her.

For one thing, Sadie was obliged to belong to several political organizations, for the Senator's promotional purposes. She disliked them, but tried to attend as many as possible. Her calendar was full with just those meetings alone.

6

Savannah had gone off to college.

Sadie thought she would curl up and die. She had fought and argued with Savannah over this, but, of course, Savannah won and off she went.

So, now, Sadie's life revolved around her phone conversations with Savannah. They talked several times during the week. And every Saturday.

Nothing interfered with her phone calls with Savannah. And certainly not her Saturday phone calls.

However, here was a Saturday luncheon, for the love of God. Who on earth had Saturday free for such a trite waste of time? Certainly not Sadie.

She already had fifteen errands to run—now this!

She wanted to be free at exactly two o'clock in the afternoon. That was the most likely chance of catching Savannah at the dorm. Savannah had chosen to attend a college across the country. Surprise! Sadie considered it a slap in the face. Of course, all of Savannah's friends had gone far away to colleges. Sadie knew it was a healthy thing, but she'd be damned if she would ever let Savannah know that. She could usually catch Savannah still asleep at noon on Saturdays. She looked forward all week for that phone call. As many times as she spoke with Savannah during the week, she needed to know she was okay on Saturdays. Silly? Not to Sadie.

Sometimes Savannah wasn't there. Ninety percent of the time she was in her dorm in a deep sleep—wanting to remain thus. Her responses to Sadie were just moans, grunts, then the heart-wrenching "I love you Mama, but please let me go back to sleep."

"I love you, too, Savannah." Then as she was telling Savannah how much she missed her and loved her, she could hear Savannah fumbling with the phone, trying to get it back on its cradle so she could get back to sleep.

Okay. It hurt a bit. But just hearing Savannah's voice, knowing she was okay, was enough.

Now, she would have to figure out a way to either leave the meeting early, or step out at exactly two o'clock to make the phone call. Damn it to hell!

Then, as if that weren't enough, and by God it was! This idiotic meeting would either cancel or cut short her shopping trip with Caroline. She was truly pissed.

Buddy walked into the room just as she was trying to gather all the items necessary for her diverse day. The gods had led Buddy in the wrong direction.

"You look beautiful, babe, glad you're going to the meeting. It's important to me."

Well, that set Sadie's blood boiling. Something Buddy really should have avoided at all costs. He never learned.

Sadie had changed purses three times. Attempting to stuff all her needs into one attractive bag. It was not possible. She needed two bags. She found one that would pass for a briefcase and one oversized bag that was presentable. She still had to leave precious items behind.

"I'm not all that thrilled to be going, Buddy, I have more important things to do."

"I'm the guest speaker, Sadie, it would make me feel better if you were there." Buddy pouted.

Oh shit! Something else she had forgotten. "Whatever makes you feel better, Buddy, I'll be there. Now please remove yourself from my presence so I can finish getting ready. You impede my thoughts and my actions by standing within two feet of me."

God! She could be such a bitch. But Buddy was like a friggin' fly closed up in a room with you on a hot day. It kept coming toward you and you were continuously having to swat at it to keep it out of your face.

Something told Sadie this was not the way 'love' should be. Note to self. Remind Savannah. When you think you want to marry someone, be sure you don't cringe and start swearing the minute you see him enter the room. You'd think that would be a given. Why had Sadie never learned this over the years?

Reluctantly, Sadie turned her attention back to Buddy. "We can't go together, Buddy, I may have to leave a little early. I have errands to run."

"Well, honey, I thought we could spend the rest of the afternoon together. I thought we could drive around, drop by to say hello to Kevin at the book store and run by the Capitol for a minute . . ."

"More politicking? Sorry, pal, I put in my time. I politic for you all week, run your headquarters, volunteer at the Veterans' Hospital, run a house, and on the weekends I need a couple of hours to do personal things. But tomorrow we can have an outing together. It's called grocery shopping. Care to join me?

Or has my company lost some of its appeal at this point?" Sadie was blunt and walking the thin line of hatefulness.

"Okay, fine." Buddy announced frantically. He was back-pedaling. No way in hell he wanted to be in on anything that did not involve his own pleasure or self-promotion—same thing. "We'll go grocery shopping tomorrow."

Sadie stared at him a minute. "We'll play your game for now. You know damned well you'll find a way out of the grocery shopping."

Sadie saw the slight grin on Buddy's face. He thought he was cute when he got caught in a little white lie. He was trying to act boyishly charming in back-tracking on his promise. God, how Sadie wished she had a gun.

"I will be leaving the meeting early." She grabbed her bags. "I'm gone. I'll see you at the luncheon. Good luck with your speech. I'll smile and applaud. You'll be proud." She merrily strolled out of the house toward her car.

"Could I have a kiss, please?" The Senator demanded, showing his irritation.

Sadie stalked back, gave him a peck, a dirty look and retraced her steps to get the fuck away from him and into her car. Freedom, of sorts. Once again, Sadie longed for that gun.

Sadie arrived at the luncheon looking elegant and sexy. She smiled at everyone, winking at some of her favorite men. She chatted with everyone she liked, patted several people on the shoulder and smiled her way hurriedly to a seat close to an exit.

"Hey, Babe!" The Senator was up near the podium. Sadie waved and under her breath hissed "Don't you dare call me up there! I've found my seat." Well this sucks out loud!

Remember Sadie's luck?

"Come up here, Sweetie, sit with me." The Senator sounded casual, but we know better, don't we?

"Sorry, dear, gotta sit here. Waiting for someone— previous plans and all. Remember?" Sadie smiled her sweetest smile and blew him a kiss. That should shut him up.

Then Sadie sat down and started going through her briefcase and purse as though she were desperate to find valuable papers, or the like. As she fumbled through her bag, she kept her eyes down. If Buddy caught her eye, she knew fire would be coming from them. How dare she defy him— publicly at that!

Finally, the president of the club called the meeting to order and Sadie could relax and look up. She felt Buddy's eyes on her, trying to intimidate her.

"Fuck you, Buddy. Nothing comes between me and my phone calls with my kid." She smiled those words at Buddy then immediately looked away again.

Her watch hit 2:00 p.m. as everyone was standing to applaud Buddy's speech. Sadie already had both bags in hand and was running for the door.

As she drove away, she saw Buddy standing in the doorway.

Hah! I got away, you selfish bastard. I'm going to call my baby, then go shopping. You go politicking with your buds. That took some maneuvering, but she had gotten away from him. She'd pay for it later, but she'd give back as good as she got.

One more point of contention in their relationship was the church going.

Sadie accompanied the Senator to church at least twice a month.

They had always gone to services semi-regularly since they started dating.

Buddy was a die-hard Baptist. Sadie was agnostic. And Savannah, Savannah had been a teenager at the time, trying whatever suited her fancy. Her fancy did not find her accompanying her mother and step-father to church. But, for political purposes, Sadie acquiesced, knowing this was a necessity. They compromised on the Episcopal Church.

Sadie would stroll into church a couple of feet in front of her husband. This was her way of showing her disrespect for him. Also, people could get a better look at her before they started lobbying around him.

Like all politicians, if they were adored, people excused their bad behavior. This irritated Sadie, hence her deliberate walk ahead of him into church and down the aisle, forcing everyone to admire her before they caught sight of their beloved Senator.

Having been raised just one step above a snake handler, Sadie wouldn't go near a Baptist church. She let the Senator know she was making a huge sacrifice by attending any church.

Caroline questioned Sadie's hypocrisy one night over drinks.

"Well, hell, Caroline, I'm agnostic, not a damned heathen!"

Caroline could use that against her at another time. Now she was intent on making her explain her much gossiped about affair.

Sadie defended herself by saying, "You know damned well I deserve this for what I put up with from that womanizing old coot!"

"You don't think the diamond earrings and diamond watch are enough?" Caroline asked.

"You get those things all the time and Wagner doesn't do a damned thing wrong! What do you think would be proper compensation for infidelity, public humiliation, and everything else I tolerate?" Sadie was about to get on her high horse and ride away.

"Okay, okay!" Caroline gave up. "It's your marriage."

"That's a cheap shot, Caroline! How dare you call this a marriage!"

The two friends were off again, laughing and talking about their favorite subjects: daughters, fashion and less informed folk than themselves.

7

Sadie found herself back in her sun room. Apparently, after throwing her hissy fit in the kitchen, all that residual resentment accompanying her walk back into history, had tired Sadie out and she had fallen asleep. She was startled awake by the phone.

Buddy was calling her from his cell phone. He had recovered nicely from his hospital stay, had had a good nap and was now going to the grocery store—could he get anything for her?

"Yes, stay gone for the rest of the day, visit your friends. Go to the Capitol. Everyone will be out of their minds with joy to see you!

"You woke me up! Don't call here again and I mean it! Stay gone!" Sadie screamed into the phone.

He apologized. She sat up and watched him drive down the driveway and away from the house.

"Son-of-a-bitch!" Sadie huffed.

She looked at the clock. It was almost noon. She got up and went to the kitchen. She wasn't hungry, so she decided she'd just have a glass of sweet tea.

Sadie took her glass of tea and went back to the sun room. Her favorite room in the house. She could sit there and look out at her beautiful garden.

God, she would hate to give up this house. She had found it, did all the decorating; she really felt as though this house belonged to her.

Oh! Wait a minute…she'd had this feeling before!

"They're all sons-a-bitches!" Sadie said with a fierceness she rarely felt.

It wouldn't work that way. It never did. Could she put up with Buddy long enough not to have to leave this house? She'd be so comfortable here, if it weren't for him.

"I've got to get over this anger." She told herself. "Maybe I'll see a therapist."

She and Buddy had tried that once together. He had lied to the therapist so much, the therapist refused to see them any more as a couple.

"Screw Buddy. I need help. That's it, it's on my list of things to do. Now, I'm going to try to be civil to that jerk when he comes home. I hope he doesn't come back too soon, though. I'll have to work my way up to civility." At least she had a plan.

"He's not responsible for all the misery in my life." Sadie continued her strategizing aloud. "He's only responsible for the misery I've experienced since I've known him."

Sadie prepared herself to call Caroline so she could let her in on the new plan. She'd let her in on the new plan, then she'd listen to Caroline laugh her ass off at today's plan, then Caroline would do a three hundred and sixty degree turn and explain to Sadie how to be civil…just to The Senator. She was an absolute angel to everyone else.

At that moment, her phone rang. It was her neighbor, Bridgette.

"I haven't seen you in forever. I saw Buddy leave. I need your company. Might I come over for a drink?"

Sadie saw Bridgette through the glass before she heard the rap on the door. Sadie dashed to open the door. Bridgette hugged her then stepped back to look at Sadie.

"You look tired and sad. I don't see that usual sparkle in your eyes. Now, how are you really, sweetie?"

Sadie gave a mock frown of annoyance.

"Did you come here to drink or to talk?"

Bridgette let out a laugh. "Okay, let's get a drink, then we'll talk."

Sadie led Bridgette, with their drinks, to the sitting room, just off the bedroom part of the sun room. As they got comfortable, tears filled Sadie's eyes. She was embarrassed and brushed them away.

"We must find something frivolous to discuss, Bridgette, I'm a tad weepy."

"We shan't have that, Sadie. You must immediately throw yourself into something to stop this. I can't bear to see you mope about. It's not like you at all, and it makes me uncomfortable, if you must know the truth. I've really missed you and couldn't wait to have a visit. You always make me laugh and feel better about things. I've needed our little visits, and I especially need it now, Sadie." Bridgette leaned forward and grasped her glass with both hands.

"Oh, Lord, Bridgette, I'm so full of myself, what on earth is wrong?"

"You know my best friend in Annapolis." Bridgette was looking down at her glass.

"Of course, Susan, what's happened to her?" Sadie moved to Bridgette's side on the love seat as she asked.

"Her husband, Sam, had a massive heart attack and died yesterday. It was sudden but not entirely unexpected. She's an absolute wreck. I'm flying up there tonight."

Sadie put her hand on Bridgette's shoulder. "Of course she's a wreck. I'm so glad you're going to be with her. Oh, I'm so sorry this has happened. She's lucky to have you. Please give her my best."

Now it was Bridgette whose eyes were tearing up. "Thank you, Sadie. I'll probably stay up there a week or so. I'm not sure what she needs or what she's going to do."

"Is there anything I can do for you or for her? Will Jan be at your house?"

Jan was Bridgette's personal assistant. She was at Bridgette's house most every day and always stayed there when Bridgette was out of town.

"Thank you, dear. Yes, Jan will be there and I'm sure she can handle anything that comes up, however, your number is at the top of my list in my desk drawer, so if she needs anything, may I have her call you?"

"I insist on it, Bridgette. Will you call me if there is anything I can do for you or Susan, or if you just need to talk, I'll be available."

"I shall and I expect you to call me should you need anything. I'll have my cell phone. Now I suppose I'll journey on back across the yards and finish my packing."

They walked arm in arm to the door as Sadie reiterated her condolences to Bridgette and to Susan. As they arrived at the door, they saw Savannah's car turning into the driveway.

Bridgette let go of Sadie's arm. "Darling, please don't mention any of this to Savannah while I'm here. Let me stay and enjoy her visit. You can tell her later. After a visit with you two, I'll be able to make my trip on a happier note."

Sadie kissed Bridgette's cheek. "Done.

"This will be an unexpected treat. You can't imagine what I said to her on the phone this morning. Half in play, and partly to punish her. She's either come out here to slap my face, or, to beg forgiveness for her lack of devotion. Let's find out together."

Savannah breezed into the room, and, as usual, filled it with smiles and sunshine. She had recovered from Sadie's early morning prank and they laughed hysterically as Savannah told the "jail" story to Bridgette.

They enjoyed a glorious couple of hours. This visit raised Sadie's spirits and momentarily distracted her from the mess she had made of her life. It was good to see Bridgette come back to her laughing, fun-loving self.

It was hard to go to those morose corners when Sadie watched Savannah's beautiful face, telling stories and laughing so hard she could barely get out the words.

"Ladies, I saw Mandy Anderson yesterday. She evidently had a disastrous facelift. Have you seen her recently?" This was so unlike Bridgette to initiate gossip, which meant it was especially good.

"I have seen her, she looks like that cat woman from New York." Savannah contributed.

"Good Lord! How does someone let that happen? Do you suppose she asked to look like that? At what point does one say 'Just stop now, while I look as though I've been permanently frightened'?" Sadie laughingly asked.

"Oh, it's worse than that!" Bridgette went on.

"She can't quite bring her lips together, nor can she shut her eyes."

"Oh, please, Bridgette, it can't be that bad."

"The hell it's not!" Savannah confirmed. "She has made a serious mistake! But she thinks she's divine. It will be years before she catches up with herself."

"Vain as I am, I'll never do it." Sadie declared.

"I've had little things done, and no one noticed." Bridgette's declaration stunned Savannah and Sadie. "One simply has to be subtle."

"Evidently, I'm mixing your drinks too strong. You're making this up. I don't need to be entertained that badly. You're just flat out lying to me!" Sadie didn't believe for a minute that Bridgette had had anything done to her face.

"Well, believe what you shall. Perhaps I'm just attempting to entertain you, or, perhaps it's true."

Bridgette smiled her beautiful smile which made Sadie and Savannah look at each other and spike an eyebrow.

"By damn. Maybe she's telling the truth." Savannah conceded.

"I feel as though I may have cheered you up a bit, so I'll run along while I've got a nice buzz on. I'll leave you and Savannah to filter through this new information. I love you both."

They all hugged and promised to get together in a couple of days.

"I'll call you" whispered Bridgette as she kissed Sadie on the cheek. "Not a word to Savannah for a little while."

Sadie smiled her assurance to Bridgette and closed the door.

Bridgette's fun stories gave Sadie and Savannah fodder for laughing and gossiping a while longer.

Savannah soon had to leave, but Sadie's mood had improved greatly, so it wasn't quite so painful to tell her daughter good bye. But, Sadie still pouted a bit.

"I wish you could stay longer, Savannah. I'll miss you when you go." Sadie whined. "And I just feel physically better when you're here."

"Are you sick, Mama? Are you hurting anywhere?" Savannah was serious, but annoyed.

"Well, no, baby. It's not that I'm sick, I just seem to breathe easier and have less aches and pains when you're with me." Sadie was begging for more attention.

Savannah gave her a quick hug and an exasperated look. She was getting sucked into her mother's manipulation. She had grown to recognize it, but in no way had she learned to defeat it.

"Put on some lipstick, Mama. You'll feel better." Savannah then hurried to her car before her narcissistic mother could react properly.

Sadie smiled, as though Savannah hadn't just insulted the hell out of her, she waved Savannah down the driveway.

"Spawn of the devil!" Sadie hissed softly as she watched her daughter disappear into the dusk. How could you love some one so much and yet there always seemed to be some friction bubbling just beneath the surface? It's probably just a mother/daughter thing.

Sadie would call her later about Bridgette's news. No need to end their visit on a downer.

Buddy was still out, no doubt holding his friends spellbound with his enthralling near-death experience. Or, perhaps, he had realized how serious Sadie was this time. Oh, how Sadie loved the peace and quiet of this house without Buddy. She was standing outside, after Savannah drove away, admiring the beautiful landscape. Lord, the gorgeous dogwoods, gardenia bushes, Carolina Jasmine climbing the fence and the magnolia trees. If you ever wonder why people stay in the South, just walk outside.

Her attention turned to her latest project.

Sadie had decided to spend a huge chunk of Buddy's money and have an elaborate apartment built above the garage. The therapist had told her to find some innocent hobbies.

When Sadie informed Buddy of her plans, she played it down by calling it a 'little garage apartment.' Buddy had no idea why she would want to do such a thing. But he wasn't going to irritate her any more by refusing.

As the 'little garage apartment' became more elaborate and expensive, Buddy really had to hold his tongue. He was a smart businessman, so he realized it was increasing the value of his home enormously. He tried not to refer to their house as 'his' home, but he really felt it belonged to him.

He finally stopped questioning Sadie about her little project. Buddy was just glad to see her in a good mood for a change. She spent so much time over there, he wondered if she was going to move in. She chose the paint colors, flooring and other details with more care than she had spent on their house, or so it appeared to Buddy.

Sadie wasn't sure herself, why she was so obsessed with getting this built. Maybe she thought she might need the money some day and rent it out. She said once it would be for the grandkids when they needed it. Lots of possibilities for its future.

8

*M*onths had passed. Buddy was still alive, showing no signs of being on his way to meet his maker any time soon. Things had quickly returned to normal, relatively speaking.

He was being honored for some wonderful thing he had done. Actually, it was to honor the Veterans, so Sadie was all for it, and even proud of Buddy for doing an honorable thing. Sadie was as patriotic as they came, so she was looking forward to going to the dedication.

Sadie was preparing her shopping trip for her dress for the event. She was financially able to shop at the most exclusive stores. She chose to shop alone on this particular occasion. Sometimes Sadie had to do things alone. Even without Caroline. This shopping trip was one of them.

Sadie still embodied so much of that little, dirt-poor girl, that sometimes it overtook her and she shut everyone out.

When she graduated high school and left home at seventeen, she had developed a sense of style on her own. With the cheapest, pitiful pieces of clothing and, sometimes, just cloth, she could manage to put together a stylish outfit. She only had, maybe three, outfits. When she was twenty-one, she could fit all of her clothes in a large paper bag. That included her two pairs of shoes, minus the ones she was wearing.

She taught herself to sew. She couldn't afford to buy magazines herself, but she would look through ones from the waiting room in the hospital where she worked. She would find a picture of a simple, elegant dress. Then she would search for inexpensive fabric on sale, as close to the color of the dress as possible. Naturally the quality of the fabric would pale considerably by comparison to the one in the picture. But Sadie would come pretty damned close as far as the overall look of the dress. She also learned to choose very inexpensive pieces of jewelry and make the most of them. Somehow, she always knew less was more, and she had an uncanny knack for knowing what looked cheap and what could pass for understated elegance.

She simply had an innate sense of fashion. She never talked with anyone about it. She didn't have a television, so no fashion shows. When she started dating, movies were a huge source of inspiration. Sadie was extremely thin, but she so desperately wanted to be curvaceous like her beautiful blonde sister. She didn't realize that because she was so thin, these simple inexpensive clothes hung beautifully on her. She knew she had to settle for the Audrey Hepburn look because her sister sure as hell had the Marilyn Monroe thing going on.

People wouldn't believe that Sadie had sewn her outfits. She would buy a cheap pair of shoes and use food coloring, shoe polish—anything she could get hold of—and dye the shoes the color she wanted. Nobody else would have anything like hers. That was important to her. Then came Wal-Mart. Sometimes she could manage to buy an item of clothing on sale there, remake it, and receive many compliments on it. She compulsively told people the entire story behind the outfit, taking away the glamour. But they didn't believe her, so no harm done.

She knew exactly how things should fit to be the most flattering to her body. She instinctively knew what length her skirt should be to best show off her legs. She always thought her legs were her best feature. She also cultivated her sexy, elegant walk and moves from women in the movies. She was seriously into becoming one of those self-assured, elegant women. She was always aware of the appearance she made when she strode into a room, and she practiced her walk until it became a stroll.

Sadie consciously practiced graciousness. Her role models were her Grandmother and her Auntie. She made a huge effort to greet everyone graciously and to speak softly. In spite of her being so aware of every move she made and the impression she made on people, she was truly kind, loving and caring. People were drawn to her sincerity and generosity. And she was great fun.

Sadie had learned at an early age from her sister and three brothers, to laugh and find humor in everything. God knows it was hard to do. But it was imperative for their survival. Thank goodness the five of them had incredible senses of humor. They were Sadie's favorite people to be around. Nobody ever made her laugh harder.

Sadie never looked at her cultivating a certain persona as being phony. She felt it was necessary to better herself. She sure as hell couldn't get a decent job if all she had were the tattered, faded hand-me-downs she was dressed in when she lived at home. So when she graduated high school at seventeen, she was out on her own. Necessity forced her to immediately become "somebody".

Her sister graduated high school at sixteen (she skipped the eleventh grade). Smart, tall, shapely and beautiful, she was turned out into the world to get a job which she did, 'toot sweet.' She helped Sadie and the brothers, of course.

Sadie couldn't afford to dwell on those years. Oh, hell, no! She tried frantically to forget it all. Some of the horror and brutality would never leave her, but with the help of some half-assed, not quite honest, psychotherapy and an early addiction to tranquilizers, she kept strolling along.

Years later, Sadie ran into an old high school boyfriend. He innocently remarked about how pretty she was in high school, even though her "clothes were too big, too long and out-of-style". He was awkwardly complimenting her, but the pain was nearly unbearable. Sadie had managed to pretend all during her school years that no one noticed. Surviving her horrific home life was a miracle in itself, but had she realized everyone noticed the way she dressed, she simply couldn't have shown up at school. Sadie had become strong, but mostly because she pretended things didn't happen.

Sadie was very popular and had a lot of friends. She was even a cheerleader. Going to cheer at the ballgames was the only place she was allowed to go that was not church-oriented. Everyone knew she was not allowed to have friends come to visit her at her home and she was rarely allowed to visit other people's homes. And she couldn't date.

Imagine what a delightful person she must have been to have her schoolmates overlook these things and still be her friend and truly enjoy her company.

Sadie never forgave the man who, thirty years after the nightmare was over, let her in on what other people saw. He never should have passed on that information to Sadie. It damaged a part of her that she had so carefully protected her entire life. Sadie refused to see him again or even talk with him on the phone. Her pride wouldn't allow her to explain to him the pain he had caused.

This incident forced her to remember vividly some of the hideous clothing she was forced to wear. She could feel her face flush remembering the sight she must have presented.

There was a hidden, sad little girl that hung around Sadie's neck all the time. She wouldn't go away. Sadie had tried to love her away through Savannah. She wasn't sure how that had worked out, but she was relatively sure it didn't have the affect she had intended.

But today, Sadie had chosen a gorgeous, elegant dark blue dress that cost more than her parents had spent raising her.

Sadie concentrated totally on the upcoming ceremonial evening. She was going to make Buddy proud. Oh, come on…to hell with Buddy! She wanted to be the star of the evening, she deserved it!

Sadie's visits with the therapists were just a continuation of her life. She was trying to impress and entertain the therapist. So she was getting nowhere. But, the practice was helping her with her acting when it came to being civil to The Senator. And, she learned a lot of good, key phrases to use in their frequent battle of words.

She was going to attempt to show admiration toward the Senator. She might be able to pull this off, because it was a tribute to the Veterans. Again, something very dear to her.

Buddy would expect her to show some affection toward him. Well, that sure as shit wasn't gonna happen. Therapy was helpful, but it wasn't magic for Christ's sake. She would have to be so dazzling, no one would notice she was repulsed by, and therefore ignoring, her husband.

As she was explaining all this to Caroline during one of their shopping days, Caroline shook her head. "Why do you have to plan to be mean to him while appearing to be devoted? You've done it for years, I thought it just came naturally."

"I don't know. It's getting more and more difficult and I feel I have to plan out every move in order to pull it off. I'm just really sick of it." Sadie admitted. "I'm such a hypocrite. I'm even losing respect for myself."

"Are you going to leave him?" Caroline asked earnestly.

Sadie became serious, causing Caroline to have a small dizzy spell and ask Sadie to wait a minute, until the feeling passed.

Sadie was a little pissed. Drama was her personal thing and Caroline usually didn't cross that line. But, she had to give her friend this moment—then she could go on and resume her rightful place in the spotlight.

"You know, I'm really going to try to hold on. I don't think I can lose this house and all my stuff. Not again. I'll have to get through this. But, I want to have my heart in it this time."

Caroline was smiling.

"Well, hell fire! I'm serious, Caroline! Can you please be supportive? You're always trying to get me to straighten up and act right. Now, I'm pouring my heart out to you and telling you I'm going to try to do all those things, and you're laughing!"

"In that case, I'm not laughing. It's hard to know when you're trying to entertain me and when you're serious."

"Damn it to hell, I am serious." Sadie put her hands on her hips and started walking across the dressing room. Caroline followed. Sadie was concentrating and ever so dramatic.

"I'm going to have to have your help." Sadie informed her friend.

"You always have my support, Sadie. You know that."

"Yes, I do. I just need you to tell me I'm not as horrible a person as I know I am."

Caroline laughed. "You're not a horrible person. You're a good person who's turned a bit jaded."

"Then stop laughing. When someone is telling me what a wonderful human being I am, laughing hysterically shouldn't be a part of it."

Sadie realized there was no way she was going to get the smile off Caroline's face. But that was okay. She knew Caroline was always in her corner. Laughing at her, yes. But, still in her corner.

9

$\mathcal{S}$adie's exquisite midnight blue dress was fitted, short, just topping the knees in length. The long sleeved, simple cut with just the right amount of décolletage, hugged her still narrow waist, nice ass and great legs. For an old broad, Sadie was a looker and she knew it.

She chose to go with her three carat diamond stud earrings, bare neck, her largest diamond rings, one on each hand. Her diamond watch and a great diamond and sapphire bracelet that Bridgette O'Shay, her next door neighbor, had forced her to borrow. When Bridgette saw Sadie's dress, she went immediately to her safe and brought forth the cuff bracelet. She handed it to Sadie. Bridgette just said "You will wear this."

Hell, Sadie wasn't about to offend a woman with a jewel collection she would share.

Sadie's shoes were barely there. Jeweled, strappy stilettos. They made her legs look even longer—carefully chosen with the knee-length dress—everyone else would be wearing long gowns.

Thank God Sadie's ensemble was chosen and in her closet by the time Savannah decided to go shopping for her own gown.

Gird your loins, folks, the usual 'mother/daughter' 'Sadie/ Savannah', 'love/hate', 'if you like it, I'm going to think it's a piece of shit' shopping trip was ON!

Sadie feared no one—except people with whom she wasn't likely to encounter. She had an irrational fear of her own fashion style being critiqued by the style icon, Anna Wintour. She also had a great fear of finding herself on Hardball being quizzed by Chris Matthews, regarding her political knowledge.

But her greatest fear was of her own daughter. She cherished Savannah, who could turn on her with the venom of the deadly coral snake. At a moment's notice. Worse — often with no notice at all. She had every reason to be afraid. Sadie supposed she should take some responsibility for Savannah's resentment, she was the one who raised her. But . . .

She stopped her car in front of Savannah's house and walked to her front door. Savannah opened the front door, looking voluptuous and sexy as usual. As Sadie opened her mouth to convey this thought to Savannah, Savannah said in a stone cold voice "I'm a fat pig. I can't leave the house, much less shop and I certainly cannot purchase clothing to put on this disgusting pig body."

When Savannah stopped talking, Sadie didn't skip a beat. "My exact thoughts, Savannah. I only came by to help you select a secluded resort where you can stay hidden for however long it takes until you can once again be seen in polite society." Sadie replied earnestly.

Savannah's facial expression did not change.

"Oh, get in the car, Mama. Let's get this shit over with."

"Hell, yeah! We're going to have fun!" Sadie exclaimed in a cheerful voice, wondering how quickly the fight would ensue.

Her schizophrenic daughter turned to her, "Where should we try first? Passions is having a sale. Shall we go there?"

"Sounds good. Who are you today, dear?" Sadie asked innocently and carefully.

"Oh, whatever, Mother!" Savannah snarled, completely dismissing the preceding conversation.

Oh, I remember her, Sadie thought. She's a pisser. We'll have a challenging day, but not without a few laughs.

First stop—Passions. Both women were greeted warmly by the saleswomen.

"Dammit, Mama, I don't want anyone seeing me try on these clothes!" Savannah whispered through clinched teeth.

"Savannah, I attempted to get all the stores to send their saleswomen home today while we shopped, so they wouldn't irritate you. Not only did they refuse to do that, but they insisted on staying in their own stores while we shop. Sorry, sugah, I tried."

Silence from Savannah as she stared straight ahead.

"Baby girl, they're not coming into the dressing room with you." Sadie tried to calm Savannah.

"Well, hell, I guess not! Like someone else could fit in the dressing room! Oh, just stop trying to make me feel better. I know I'm a fat cow. People will be looking and pointing." Savannah was roughly shoving aside each gown on the first rack, her mood becoming blacker second by second.

"I'll come into the dressing area with you and block the hall. No one can get past me to spy on you. I'll destroy them and their families should anyone try." Sadie promised.

Savannah tried on the first gown as Sadie stood outside the dressing room.

"Son-of-a-bitch!" Loudly, from the dressing room. "How the fuck can anybody get this damned fat and still live? If I can get this piece of shit off of me, we're going home! But it won't come off! Dammit, Mama, I'm stuck in this fucking dress!"

Sadie rolled her eyes. "Good God." She said softly, then to Savannah.

"Shall I come in and help?"

"Hell, no! I'll rip this off before I let anyone see me in it."

Then there was just a slew of the most foul words Sadie had ever heard or used, for that matter, spewing from her beautiful daughter's mouth.

"Hand it to me. I'll hand you this next one. It's quite beautiful."

"I've got to get out of here. Grab this thing. I'm kicking it under the door."

"I've got it. Now, take this one." Sadie grabbed the discarded dress and laid the next one over the dressing room door.

"It can't be done, Mama!"

"Cowboy up, Sissy! We're on a mission. You don't have any choice. Try just this one more dress to pacify me. Then, we'll leave."

"Damn right, we will." Savannah hissed. Still swearing and huffing about, Savannah took the dress. Sadie could hear nothing as Savannah pulled the beautiful white silk jersey dress up her body. Sadie then heard the hidden side zipper being zipped up. Still no sound from Savannah.

"Darlin'? Are you still in there? There better not be a window you've crawled out of."

"You wanna come in, Mama?" Savannah asked quietly.

"Sure, can I fit in there?" Sadie was pleased when she heard Savannah stifle a giggle at her mother's teasing.

Sadie opened the door to a vision. The dress was strapless and body-clinging. Cut on the bias, reminiscent of the glamorous 40's. A small bit of rouching at the bust line. It was flattering to Savannah's beautiful shoulders, breasts, ass and long shapely legs—all on display.

"God Almighty, Savannah, you are a knockout." Sadie gasped. She was spellbound by Savannah's beauty. "You're body was made for that dress." Sadie continued to stare.

Savannah was also staring at herself in the mirror. Once again the fury and anger between the two was laid aside—as though it had never occurred.

"Well, I must say, I do wonders for this little number." Savannah smiled with delight, as she turned to see herself from every angle. "Perhaps I can be seen in public after all. But not until I find the perfect shoe!"

"You know what, baby girl, that dress looks so good, let's get two shoes." Sadie was giddy with joy at Savannah's pleasure with her dress.

"Get over yourself, Mama. It's all about me, now. I know the exact shoe I must have and I have also envisioned the diamond drop that must fall exactly here!" Savannah was pointing to a spot just before her breasts were prepared to spill from the top of the white silk jersey creation.

Sadie's heart soared to see Savannah so happy. But wait just a damned minute. Did you hear that last part? Savannah has envisioned the shoes and the drop necklace. What were the chances some designer has magically created precisely what this unpredictable (unless the earth suddenly takes a slight turn to the left so as not to piss off Savannah) 'devil woman' has just this instant envisioned?

Now, it's coming. The hunt for the impossible. The shoes and diamond drop, which Savannah had just this instant conjured up in her mind's eye.

Sadie surreptitiously reached into her purse for her pillbox. She fished out two calm-me-downs.

Savannah caught her and laughed "You're gonna need those, Mama, I'm on a roll."

I won't even need water for these suckers, thought Sadie as she dry-swallowed the pills.

10

*T*he day had finally arrived. And, Sadie was constantly adjusting her thoughts to portray her new lease on life. This wasn't going to be as easy as she had anticipated.

As the big night arrived, she had her act down to a fine art. The Senator seemed to be buying it. He was so proud of her.

There were a couple of cocktail events leading up to the actual dedication ceremony. Sadie wasn't looking forward to that. How drunk would Buddy get before the presentation? He really needed to show some dignity and respect on this occasion.

Sadie was maintaining her self-control rather well. The therapy was helping. She was embarrassed by the hatred she spewed out weekly to the therapist regarding Buddy, but it was good for her.

Buddy was delighted with her new found sweetness, but was, understandably so, a little unnerved by it all. And quite suspicious. Sadie hadn't told him she was seeing a therapist to enable her to tolerate him. Just another little something she felt it necessary to keep from him.

But, tonight, she was an angel and would ignore him as best she could. She could be The Senator's wife without spending every minute with the man.

Election was coming up in a year. God knows why, but he was going to make another run at it. He would win, no doubt. He had been a excellent Senator and this would definitely be his last time out. Six more years and he would be too old to run again.

So, she would have to be devoted during this next year. She could barely think about it, but, hell, she'd been through it before and she was a dream wife for a candidate. Buddy was so in awe of her charisma, and appreciative of her—until the election was over, then he was his miserable self again. But at least he was gone a lot. That helped things tremendously.

Tonight she could dream-walk through her perfect wife's roll.

They were leaving the limousine, and walking up the steps of the Capitol. Buddy reached for Sadie's hand and she took it, smiling at him like a new lover. The cameras were everywhere. She was in her element.

The crowd was roaring. Sadie and the Senator weren't the only politicians en route to the party at the Capitol. The Governor and his wife were ahead of them. She saw the Attorney General and his wife within arms' reach. But Sadie pretended the clapping and yelling was all for her—or the Senator and his wife, of course.

Everywhere, red, white and blue balloons were floating in the air, popping occasionally and annoying the hell out of Sadie. There was a sudden pop very near her ear. Damn, she hated those friggin' balloons! She jumped at the sound and felt Buddy's hand tighten on hers. There were so many people, they seemed to be crushing in. Sadie started walking, almost running, up the steps, trying to push her way through the crowd. She hated crowds and was quickly becoming claustrophobic.

She was trying to get away from the swarm of people. Buddy's hand was too tight on hers and she tried to shake it loose.

The aides, friends, police and capital security—it was all just too much! Sadie couldn't breath.

"Get away!" Sadie yelled to no one and everyone, as she continued to push her way up the steps and away from the crowd.

She had shaken loose from Buddy. The crowd was getting louder. Suddenly a man grabbed her, put his arm around her shoulder and ran with her, pushing the crowd out of her way, up the steps and, finally, into the Capitol. He pushed her into a side room.

Once they were inside, Sadie turned around to assess just what in the hell was going on. Who had had the unprecedented gall to interfere in her night? Her entrance, nonetheless—the most important part!

Sadie first focused on the man who had grabbed her and gotten her out of harm's way. She turned to the man and said, "Oh, thank you! I am so claustrophobic, I couldn't bear another moment out there."

The man was looking at her and all around them. Then Sadie noticed the pistol in his hand.

Sadie screamed and turned to run. The man grabbed her.

"Capital Security, Mrs. Montgomery. I have to get you to a secure location."

"Why?" Sadie asked, confused, but not scared.

"Did you hear a gun shot out there?"

"No! Those damned balloons popping was all I heard!" Sadie was irritated and wasn't quite processing what the officer was insinuating.

"There was also a gun, Mrs. Montgomery." The officer said as he was watching Sadie's face. He was a seasoned police detective, trained to protect and read people. And he had no idea what was going through Sadie Montgomery's mind at that moment.

Other people were now pouring in through the doors. She saw the Governor and his wife being hurried off to a private room.

"I wonder who had a gun? Well, that was stupid. Do I have to stay here until they get him? Can you take me to the room where the party is? I'm sure the Senator is waiting for me." Sadie was obviously not comprehending the situation. The detective took a deep breath before he addressed her again.

"I need you to stay here for a moment." The detective told her.

Three more detectives and one of the Senator's aides came in at that time. The aide walked directly to Sadie and took her arm. The first detective left the room. Another agent asked, "Mrs. Montgomery, how close did the gun shot sound to you?"

"What the hell are you talking about? I thought a balloon had popped!" She was looking out the glass door, she had lost sight of everyone. She hadn't seen her husband, or Savannah and Beau…had everyone wandered off with friends? Had she lost them all when she started rushing up the steps to get inside?

Where were Caroline and Wagner? What the hell? If they left me here, I'll have every one of their hides!

Suddenly, she saw Caroline's red dress through the door. She ran to the door, opened it, and yelled, "Caroline! Come here!"

All the men in the room, Aides and Security, made a dive for Sadie.

"What the hell is wrong with ya'll?" She was mad as a hornet.

She managed to get hold of Caroline, somehow, and pulled her in the room with her as the men pulled Sadie back.

"Mrs. Montgomery, we need to talk with you, alone. Immediately," one of the men said. At this point, Sadie didn't recognize anyone other than Caroline.

"No, you don't! This is my best friend, Caroline Herrington. She can hear anything you have to say." By that time, Sadie had had the time to see Caroline from head to foot. "Why do you always have to have a more expensive dress than anyone else? That can just be tacky in some situations, Caroline."

Caroline stared at Sadie.

"Sadie, are you okay?" Caroline asked.

Buddy's aide whispered to Caroline. "We haven't told her yet. They are trying to question her, to see if she saw anyone with a gun and how close the shot sounded."

Caroline put her arm around Sadie in an attempt to pull her away.

"Don't try to suck up now, Caroline. You know your dress is more attention-getting than . . . ." Sadie was interrupted.

"Mrs. Montgomery!" One of the agents spoke up, sternly.

"What is your problem?" Sadie snapped back. "I need to get to the party or my husband is going to be furious with me!

Is this whole shooting thing over with now? Why are we still here?"

"Oh, good Lord." Caroline was shaking her head.

At that point, all Sadie could do was look around. It was finally hitting her that there was something amiss. "Welcome to the party." Caroline thought to herself, as she saw that her friend was beginning to realize this wasn't an attempt to keep her from the benefit.

"Mrs. Montgomery," the aide started, "the Senator was hit by a bullet! He's been taken to the hospital. The agents got you in here and out of the way for safety's sake.

"We'll take you to the hospital now. But an agent will have to ride with you. They need to ask you what you saw and heard. We want to know if there is any carbon deposit on your clothes, how close the gun was to you."

Caroline immediately started speaking for Sadie. She was horrified at the way they had just disclosed this information to Sadie. She tried everything she could to get into that car to go with Sadie, short of physical assault on one of the security agents. But, they were adamant. Sadie begged Caroline to find Savannah and let her know what was going on.

"Honey, Savannah knows what's going on, everyone knows what's going on except you! Now go to the hospital. Savannah's probably already there and I'm right behind you!" Caroline gave the agent a snub as she walked past.

In the limousine, on the way to the hospital, the agents questioned Sadie as though they had found the smoking gun in her hand. By the time they got her to the hospital, she wanted to get out of their sight so she could check her purse, maybe she did have a gun in there.

Sadie was ushered into an emergency room cubicle. They were working on the Senator. He wasn't conscious.

He had been shot in the head. The bullet had been retrieved at the scene. It was from a small hand gun which had been fired at fairly close range. Sadie still couldn't believe what was happening around her. She had no blood on her, The Senator hadn't fallen…Well, she didn't see him, she was too busy trying to get the hell out of that damned crowd! Maybe that's why they were treating her like she had shot her own husband. Screw them!

She would normally be dripping honey around the handsome policemen and detectives, or whatever they were. Tonight, she was too pissed to drip honey on anybody! Oh wait! Concern, Sadie. Concern. She had to remind herself to show concern for her husband's well-being, at least in front of all these people. God! What a bitch I am. Sadie had finally caught a glimpse of Buddy through the hospital staff and security agents surrounding him. He really is hurt!

Where the hell was Savannah? Sadie felt the anxiety rising. Where the hell was Caroline? How dare they keep me from my daughter and my best friend?

"I heard a balloon pop. Damn it!" She heard herself screaming, but she couldn't stop. She no longer cared to whom she was yelling.

"The crowd was crushing and I jerked loose from the Senator and went as quickly as I could up the steps. A man came up, put his arm around my shoulder and hurried me into a room in the Capitol.

"That's what I know! I don't intend to repeat it one more time!" She looked around. It seemed everyone had focused their attention away from Buddy and on her. It was about damn time!

There. She had had her public hissy fit and now she stormed down the hall into the ladies' room. She stared at herself in the mirror. Guards had followed at a respectful distance. They waited outside.

"What's happening here?" she asked her reflection.

"I look fabulous, I'm supposed to be at a party. A party for which I have spent weeks preparing! Now that son-of-a-bitch has done it again. The bastard's been shot. My husband, the one I keep threatening to kill. Oh, shit! I've got to get the hell out of here." Sadie had finally processed what was going on. She took a deep breath, and one more look in the mirror.

She walked out of the ladies' room, holding her head high. She walked down the hall, oblivious to the guards following close behind, back to where she had left their entourage. That's when the lights hit her. News cameras were everywhere. They were yelling at her asking how the Senator was, where he had been shot, was he going to live? Had she heard the shot?

Suddenly, an aide appeared from nowhere and pulled her into a waiting room and shut the door on the media and their cameras.

"Thank you, David. Sorry about turning into a screaming banshee. Have I lost my mind, or are we back in the hospital with the Senator?"

"I'm sorry, too, but yes. We're back in the hospital. But this time it's a bit more serious, Sadie."

"Where's Savannah? David, I need to see my daughter! Where is Caroline? She was with me and they just pulled me away from her at the Capitol. Wouldn't even let her come with me. The nerve of those bastards."

"Everything's a nightmare right now, Sadie. No one knows what to do or what the hell has happened."

"The place was crawling with policemen, detectives and guards. How could anyone get close to him? I only saw security and aides. And the Governor and his wife. It was probably that old jackass that shot him." Sadie looked up at David, the Senator's aide. He wasn't laughing.

"Lighten up, David. Find out what's going on with Buddy. I am always inappropriate when I'm nervous." Sadie started fiddling around, apparently trying to open her purse. Then she looked back up at David as he was leaving the room.

"You'll be safe in here, Sadie," David assured her. "But do me one favor, please…stay here, Sadie. Don't leave this room right now, and don't do anything…you would normally do." David was shaking his head, there was no time for being politically correct right now, not even to the Senator's wife.

"David, wait." Sadie said before he could escape her company. "Do they really think I had something to do with this?"

"Nobody really knows what to think right now. Let's try not to put any ideas in their heads, okay?" David tried to let out a small smile. He turned and left the room.

Sadie shrugged and, after finally managing to open her purse, it was new after all, she took out her cell phone and called Savannah. Savannah reported she was almost to the hospital.

Then she called Caroline. She was already in the parking lot Caroline told her, she just couldn't figure out how to get inside.

Against David's suggestion, Sadie slid out another door and got the attention of a policeman she hadn't yet encountered. Or, as she knew was more advantageous to the circumstances, he hadn't yet encountered her. Sadie sent him out to find Caroline and bring her in and to have them on lookout for Savannah. She wanted her brought to her immediately.

Caroline finally came into the waiting room. She hugged Sadie.

"Everything's all right. Buddy will be fine, let's go see what the doctor has to say."

Sadie sighed and showed how tired she was. "Oh, Caroline, they won't even let me talk to a doctor. They're stabilizing him. As if I care.

"They're also questioning me like I shot him." Caroline should have been taken aback by how quickly the change took place in Sadie's voice, but she was rather used to it. Sadie went on, as usual.

"They have asked me every move I've made since I picked out my damned dress. A dress that has completely gone to waste, by the way." Sadie looked to ensure her joke had not escaped Caroline. It hadn't.

"They also asked me where you got that magnificent red dress that was so inappropriate, being that you're the best friend of the Senator's wife. Good Lord, Caroline, this jealously thing is out of control. Have you considered therapy?"

This time, Caroline laughed out loud. "Sadie, you're crazy. But this dress must really look good. You can't seem to shut-up about it."

"Thank God I didn't get any blood on this gorgeous blue number. I consider it never having been worn in public since no one saw me."

"You're all over the television, and you'll be all over the television and newspapers tomorrow, and probably a few more days. You might as well write that one off as a charitable donation. It has been worn and seen."

Sadie was still on a roll regarding lecturing Caroline about competing with her. "Jealousy is such an ugly thing, Caroline. It's so beneath you. But, of course, I understand it. I'm generous that way."

Sadie was having such a good time berating Caroline and attempting to deny reality, that Caroline let her ramble on.

"I'm not quite sure how to feel about this media attention. Of course, any publicity is good publicity. Am I right, Caroline?"

"You're always right, Sadie, and no one knows how to play the media better than you do."

"Oh! Now you're just being a bitch. It hurts me so to see you turn into that snide, snippy twit that you slip into so easily." Now Sadie was giggling at herself. Caroline laughingly congratulated Sadie on being the craziest person in the world. Sadie was wallowing in the compliment when they were abruptly rushed off to the ICU where Buddy was.

Dr. Rush came out with scrubs on. He took his surgical cap off and was removing his gloves.

"Sadie, come here and sit down," he instructed. "I need to give you an update." Caroline squeezed Sadie's hand and led her to some chairs.

They sat down with the doctor. He explained how the bullet had struck his skull tangentially, it was a perforating wound. The wound caused laceration and crushing and had displaced the tissue in it's track. Hitting the bone had deflected the bullet causing less damage. They had him on an intravenous drip of antibiotics...

Buddy is sixty-five, not exactly old, but old enough to cause his recovery to be slower. His blood pressure was very low. They were medicating him so he would sleep for awhile.

Sadie was only listening to every third word or so, not knowing what most of them meant. She had heard enough to know that Buddy was probably going to live. Dr. Rush went on to tell Sadie that Buddy's chances were good at this point. They were mostly worried about infection. He then gently patted Sadie on the shoulder and left her with his private pager number.

There was still commotion all around. The Senator's aides and outer edge friends were showing their respect yet keeping their distance. Sadie could thank Caroline for that. She probably wouldn't, but she could have. Sadie would have done the same thing for Caroline if the tables were turned, that wasn't a secret. The protective instinct came naturally for the two.

Sadie knew what she had to do. She caught David's eye and he came over to her. Sadie told him everything Dr. Rush had told her, so he could release the information to the press, a horde of them were waiting.

David thanked her. She was the perfect political wife. Suddenly, all her craziness was forgotten. He would forgive her anything. When she put the Senator's political life at the top of everything, it made David's life so easy. Then she smiled that pretty smile, winked and turned to walk away with her friend.

My God, she's good. He looked at the crowd waiting for his medical report. They had seen Sadie talking to the doctor. They had seen Sadie immediately call David over and give him the report. Now, he had game. She had let everyone know how important he was. He wouldn't forget the favor Sadie had bestowed upon him.

Caroline and Sadie continued their walk down the hall toward the restrooms. "Do you think I did it, Caroline?"

"I think you're sorry you weren't the one who did it." The two laughed. Caroline was still laughing, but the words she said next were meant to be taken seriously.

"You've got to stop saying things like that. Especially where people can hear you. Not everyone knows you're crazy—in a good way."

"Oh, God! Savannah will go to the police and turn me in for sure this time. Remember how she tried to get me brought up on charges before?"

"Sadie, you are exaggerating. You know you are. Do you also know you're your own worst enemy?" Caroline asked, expecting no serious answer. She wasn't disappointed.

"If you're going to sit here and lecture me all night, I'm going to point the finger at you. Where is Wagner? Did he see where you hid the gun?"

"He, Lucy and the kids went home! Oh, here comes Savannah and Beau!"

"Stay with me, Caroline. She'll jump my ass about this for sure. She hates me, you know."

"Stop it, Sadie!"

"Oh, I love this. She can treat me any damned way she wants to. I'm at her mercy. I see her when she deems to give me an audience and you are on her side."

Caroline stared Sadie down until she paused for a breath. Then Caroline opened the door of the waiting room and let Savannah and Beau in.

They rushed to Sadie, hugging her, asking if she was all right and wanting to know every detail about Buddy's condition.

"Who did this, Mama?" Came the ridiculous question from Savannah.

"See Caroline? I told you. She'll have me behind bars by dawn."

"God, Mama! I meant, who could have done this."

"Sorry, I don't know. No one I hired came through for me last year, so I'm thinking it was none of them." Sadie was slowly getting pissed.

Oddly, so was Savannah.

Caroline stepped up. "Sadie, please stop. No one knows who could have done such an awful thing." Caroline then turned her authority toward Savannah.

"As your mother was saying earlier, she tends to say inappropriate things when she's nervous. Obviously, she is very nervous right now. Let's try not to make things worse."

Savannah's eyes teared up and she walked over and put her arm around Sadie. "I'm sorry, Mama."

"I'm sorry too, Savannah. Just please, don't suggest to anyone I tried to kill Buddy. Please."

Savannah, nostrils flaring with hostile frustration, was still trying to keep from crying. "I would never . . . ."

"Tick-a-lock." Sadie sat down and closed her eyes.

"I'm just too tired, Savannah. Fun as it would be to continue these little quips, I'm just too tired."

The tension was palpable. Savannah said to everyone and to no one, "I'm not helping. I'll just leave."

Sadie opened her eyes but stared into space and did not react. She was hurt bad and she knew she was carrying this too far. Why was she pushing Savannah away when she needed her so much right now?

"I'll talk to the doctor and nurses then I'll go on. I'll check later." Savannah then turned to Caroline. Caroline reached out and hugged Savannah tight to her.

"I'll call if there is any change." She told Savannah. "I'm going to stay with her for a while. She'll be okay. She must be in shock. She would never be that angry with you."

Tears were flowing freely down Savannah's cheeks now, but she was still able to manage a laugh at Caroline's attempt to console her. Caroline rolled her eyes and smiled back at Savannah. It was an understood acknowledgement of Sadie's tendency for the dramatic. And the sarcastic.

Savannah and Beau went over and kissed Sadie on the cheek and left. Sadie continued to stare into space, non-responsive. She was punishing herself as much as she was punishing Savannah. She couldn't stop herself.

"That didn't go as well as you may think it did." Caroline was beginning to wonder if Sadie had become catatonic.

"She doesn't care about me. I told you, Caroline, she hates me. She should hate me. I'm a rotten mother, always have been."

Caroline was quiet for a moment. But only for a moment.

"Sadie, you haven't always seemed to be able to make the right decisions . . . ."

Sadie interrupted, rather loudly, before Caroline had a chance to finish what she was about to start.

"Oh, for the love of God, of course I can make the right decisions, I just have to make all the other ones first. Is it just me? I thought it was just that chaotic Southern state of mind. I'm confused. No, hold on, I'm not so sure about that. Oh hell, it is just me.

"I'm not okay, am I? This is going to be the rest of my life—just like the beginning. I haven't the foggiest notion as to what the fuck I should do. Crazy's got nothing on me, Kiddo. I'm not right. It's not going to heal up, Caroline. I guess I'll just go with it. There's something bad wrong with my mind. I screw up on purpose." Sadie was hiding her face in her hands and quietly sobbing.

"You're going to be okay, Sadie. You've been under so much strain, I don't know how you function at all. Savannah knows how much you love her. Things will be back to normal the next time you see her."

"Normal is not in my vocabulary. For fifty-five years I've been waking up thinking 'Today, I'll heal up, I'll feel like a human. Today something will go my way. I'll do something sensible.' Well guess what! I try to be good. I've even, on occasion, tried to do the Lord's work. Okay—I've gone too far—but I try to do the right thing. It's not working!"

"It will, Sadie. You're good. Good things will happen. I know it."

"Caroline, if you get any more saintly on me, I'll have you tossed out of here on your ass. I think I'm going to collapse. I need a vacation from my life, I really am on the brink of a major breakdown. I don't care what happens to Buddy. Caroline, I really don't. In fact, I never want to see him again."

"Okay, don't say those things in front of anyone else. You need some rest and you're in shock. I'll talk to a doctor and see if we can't get you something. I'll take you home with me, and you can get some rest."

"I don't think they'll let me leave. But even if they do, how bad am I going to look? I have to stay here and continue the vigil. It would be inappropriate if I left. But you need to go on. There is no need for you to miss your rest. I'll ask them to find a room for me to sleep in. They'll do that. You just go on. I'm better off by myself. I shouldn't be allowed around humans. I make everyone miserable."

Caroline rolled her eyes slightly as she gave Sadie a hug.

"Can I bring you some things from your house?" Caroline wouldn't stop until she could go out of her way to help. Regardless of Sadie's gratuitous drama.

"Okay. Some panties, a robe and my cutest outfits…and all of my make-up and my shampoo, and all of the drugs in the house. You'll find them mostly in my bathroom off the sun room. You'll need a large bag.

"Now—are you happy? That'll keep you busy the rest of the night."

Caroline went over and hugged Sadie again. "I'll be back with your stuff. I'll tell the Senator's aide you need a room to rest in."

"Thank you, Caroline. I'm sorry I'm crazy." Sadie hadn't moved.

"You'll get better," Caroline said as she left Sadie alone.

Sadie didn't move. She was in the same spot, just staring, when Caroline returned a couple of hours later.

"My God, Sadie! Hasn't anyone been in to see about you? I told the aide that you were in here and needed a room so you could rest."

"Caroline, they don't care. Thanks for bringing all that stuff. I'm going to stay down at that hotel for patients' families. I can have my privacy and still be here. I'll tell them. Will you go with me and help me get settled?"

"Of course. We'll go find David." Caroline had Sadie by the shoulders, steadying her as they walked.

They found David and left word at the ICU nurses' station the room and the phone number Sadie would be staying in at the hospital's hotel.

Caroline helped her get settled. When she left, Sadie showered and got in the bed. She felt free and relaxed—she fell asleep right away.

11

*T*he phone woke Sadie at 8:30 the next morning. It was Caroline. "Sadie, I'm at the hospital. I know you're exhausted and I wanted to let you rest, but I knew you would want to be here before people started asking questions. I told the nurse you had gone to the bathroom, so just come on in the ICU waiting room when you're ready. I indicated you were nauseous. You know how your nerves are."

"Thanks for covering my ass. I don't know when I've slept so soundly. Do I have to come down there?"

"Get your make-up on and hurry. I don't like these people any more than you do. By the way, since you asked, the Senator is the same."

"If anyone asks, pretend I did ask. Thanks again, I'm on my way."

Sadie hung up and started the shower.

Damn, I could get used to this living alone and not having people bother me. Maybe I'll make Caroline stay there and cover for me and I'll hang out here at the hotel for a few days. Oh, to dream.

Sadie arrived at the hospital looking and feeling more rested than she had in years.

"Did you have a face lift after I left last night?" Caroline greeted Sadie. This would be the biggest compliment she was ever going to get from Caroline.

"Oh, thank you! Now it's going to be hard for me to act worried."

"Sadie, come on. You know you're worried."

Sadie didn't answer Caroline, they started walking toward the nurses' station to ask all the questions. Sadie felt totally detached from the situation. She wasn't curious about who had shot the Senator, or why. She wasn't even particularly interested in his condition. So much for her therapy sessions. She knew people were assuming she was in a state of shock— she would take advantage of this and guide them along in their assumptions. Caroline even thought Sadie was in distress. She would never believe Sadie was so indifferent to the situation.

A nurse came out and went back to the waiting room with them. They weren't supposed to go into ICU. The nurse explained that the Senator had had a comfortable night. They didn't think there was going to be any permanent damage, but it would be another twenty-four hours before they could be more definite. They wanted to keep him sleeping for a while longer, but Sadie could go in and sit with him if she wanted. And, finally, that the sooner he was alert and talking, the better.

Sadie allowed the nurse to have her opinion on that.

Sadie knew the right thing to do was to go into Buddy's room for a moment, to pretend an interest and concern. She did that. She even leaned over and gratuitously kissed his forehead for the consumption of the gawking nursing staff.

She came back out of his room as though she didn't want to stay too long in order not to disturb him, and headed back to the waiting room.

There were three uniformed policemen and David, the Senator's loyal aide, in the waiting room already. They were wandering about, coming in and out and walking the hall.

Sadie went up to them and gushed her appreciation. She gave David a hug. Then she and Caroline went to a corner and sat down.

"I'm not going to do this everyday, Caroline. I don't give a damn what people think any more."

Caroline looked at Sadie a minute and said, matter-of-factly, "I'm supposed to work today, but I called in. So today you and I will stay here and act right. Then we'll see."

Sadie had no comeback.

"I'm hungry, Caroline. Do we have to eat at the hospital cafeteria? Oh, never mind—I remember, that's the place for everyone to see me not leaving my husband's side."

"I'm ignoring you, Sadie. But we don't have to eat at the hospital cafeteria."

"Oh, but we shall! The food's wonderful, and they do have all the four Southern food groups."

"What are those, Sadie?" Caroline asked with genuine curiosity.

"Sugar, salt, grease and alcohol."

"Did you just make that up?"

"Nope, I've always known that. But I'm pretty sure they don't serve alcohol in the cafeteria."

"Let's go anyway." Caroline suggested.

"You're always so sensible, Caroline."

"Do I look fabulous? You did good putting my outfits together. Thank you again, if I haven't properly fallen all over myself praising you."

"You did fine. Yes, you look fabulous. Lucky for you, I have such good fashion sense."

"And I don't?" Sadie was offended.

"Good grief, Sadie, you purchased your outfits. Obviously, you have good taste. Don't get crazy on me now."

"Too late. Let's stay at the cafeteria until visiting time at ICU is over. They'll page me if they need me, won't they?"

"I'm sure they will. But we'll tell them where we're going."

Sadie was off on another tangent.

"Did you notice the Governor hasn't given the Senator so much as a by-your-leave? Who the hell does he think he is? He sure sucks up when he's running for something."

Caroline was calm. "They have him surrounded by uniformed security and plain clothes detectives. They can't let him go wandering about until they know who the man was trying to kill."

"Or woman," Sadie interjected.

"What?" This was a new one for Caroline.

"Well, really, Caroline. It's likely several women would want to kill Buddy. God knows I—"

"I told you not to say that!" Caroline was harsh and meant to be so.

"Well, la-de-damned-da," retorted Sadie. "Now you are riding off on your high horse!"

"I just don't want you to get in trouble."

Sadie looked up and saw David entering the cafeteria. He looked around until he spotted Sadie, then he started toward her table.

"What are they going to bother me with this time?"

"Be nice," Caroline said softly.

"As if!" Sadie pretended shock that Caroline would, once again, need to caution her.

David arrived at their table and apologized for interrupting.

"The Governor and his wife are at the ICU. They came to check on the Senator. You need to come up and have pictures taken with them."

"Like hell I do! He thinks he can just waltz in here any time and I'm supposed to hop-to, act like the President's come callin'? I don't think so! I don't feel like coming back upstairs. Caroline and I were finally able to force ourselves to come down and eat. I'm not budging!"

The aide gave Sadie a horrified look.

"Sadie! You have to come back up with me."

"No, I don't. I didn't even vote for the son-of-a-bitch. He's here for a photo opportunity! How rude! He can't stand that the attention is off him, now that they've figured out the Senator was the target.

"Well, they got him. Now the Governor needs to get his ass back to his office and get to work. She needs to go have her nails done...or something. She is so superficial. Tell her I said so."

"Oh Lord, Sadie," David and Caroline chorused.

"I'm in shock. Go tell them that. I think it would be unseemly of me to go up there and be photographed smiling and shaking hands. That's absolutely vulgar. See? I'm a better politician than all of them. They better hope I never decide to run against either of them."

David whispered to Caroline, "Is she drunk?"

"I wish she had that excuse. I really do think she's in shock. She's been acting like this since he got shot."

"Oh, hell," Sadie interrupted. "Don't discuss my sanity behind my back. I have been through a traumatic experience. I think I asked to see a doctor and no one complied. Thanks anyway. I'll get through this on my own. Now, please go back up and relay my message to the Governor and his wife. I mean it."

Sadie finished her speech and turned her back to David.

Caroline and David exchanged shrugs and David left the cafeteria to make up some story explaining why Sadie was indisposed.

Actually, he was tempted to use her exact words. But he had better sense. If the Governor wanted to pay his respects, he could do it without cameras. Sadie was right. It would look bad for her to be posing for pictures. She was good. She knew better.

Caroline was looking at Sadie, trying to determine if she had just suffered a stroke. No. It was just pure "Sadie." "What do you need, Sadie? Do you need to see a doctor?"

"Yes, Caroline, I do. And I need a long rest. Do you know they took my new blue dress to check it for gun powder? I made them check my hands, too. They acted like it wasn't necessary, but I think they wanted to see if I had shot a gun."

"When did they do that?" Caroline didn't know when they had the opportunity.

"Sometime after I got here, at the hospital. I made them bring my dress right back.

"Yep! They think I shot him. Well, they don't anymore. But they think I had something to do with it. I don't think I did…actually I don't even believe anything happened to him. He's just laying his ass up there to keep getting attention."

"What doctor do you want to see?" Caroline had such an irritating way of sticking to the subject.

"I'm already seeing a therapist. She knows I want Buddy dead. I guess I need to see someone to help me sleep. I love being over at the hotel, by myself. I could live there and just sleep and rest 'til Buddy's gone."

"Oh Sadie! You can't say those things to people!"

"Okay. I'll pretend to be in shock and I can't speak. You tell them what I need except, leave out the 'I need Buddy to die' part."

"Yeah, Sadie, I'll leave that part out. But first let's get you back to that room you love so much. I think it's time for you to get a little rest, I'll go tell the nurses."

Caroline passed Savannah coming into the waiting room Sadie had commandeered as her own, on her way out to give the instructions.

"Brace yourself, child. She's never been up against anything like this before. Cut her as much slack as you can." Caroline whispered her heed to Savannah as she hugged her and then walked away.

Savannah sat down next to her mother. They hugged and kissed each other, as though the tension from the night before had never happened.

"Tell me the truth, Savannah, they think I did it, don't they?"

"No, but they kind of suspect you just might have an idea of who did."

"That is such a crazy-ass thing. You know I would have done it myself. That's a pleasure I would not have passed on to anyone else," Sadie said proudly.

"Okay Mama, that's what I'm talking about. And what I suspect Caroline has talked to you about, too. You can't say those things to . . . ."

"Girl, you've got to get a sense of humor. Caroline knows I wouldn't say these things to 'anyone else but y'all'," Sadie finished Caroline's mantra in a sing-song voice, "and my therapist."

Sadie couldn't admit to herself that she was truly out of control. She could joke about being out of control, but Savannah and Caroline had just as much as confirmed it— Sadie was not handling this well.

"Why don't you know it, Buttons? I would confess if I had done it. I would be proud and, I really think my therapist would see it as a breakthrough, too."

"I wonder who did shoot him." Savannah said this more to herself.

"I guess I'm a little curious, but very little. I'm telling you, I think it's a woman. I'm sorry you have to hear all this, Savannah, but if it's my ass on the line, I'm not going to cover for that sorry shit just so you can have a father figure to look up to. Can you handle it?" Sadie waited for Savannah to respond. She did with wide eyes and a nod. Savannah wasn't quite as naïve as her mother thought. She was, however, quite anxious to hear what her mother had to say.

"God only knows what he had going on and with whom. It's not as though he is particular about the emotional and mental stability of his women. He is also likely to have promised several women he was going to leave me, and marry them. That could have pissed off any one of them. All they had to do was ask. I would have given him up, but I would insist on being paid this time."

Savannah had been watching and listening to Sadie so intently, she hadn't noticed a man, not far from her age, entering the room.

Sadie stopped talking when she sensed the presence of someone else. They both looked up.

Sadie said quickly, "Hi, Jim Wilson. Please come on in. Savannah, Jim is with the Gazette. Jim, this is my daughter, Savannah. How did you get past the big guns? I thought they were keeping me safe from dangerous men."

Sadie had slowly drifted into her flirtatious mode. Her daughter rolled her eyes. Secretly wishing she hadn't missed out on that gene.

"I just brazenly walked past everyone. They didn't pay attention. But now, after listening to your logical scenario, I'm very interested in whodunit. What you said makes a lot of sense. So, you think it might have been a woman?"

"Yes, I do. I'm so clever! Do you think I've solved it already? Savannah, did you hear that?" Sadie appeared delighted with herself.

"Maybe we can solve it together. I've been placed on police beat at the paper, at my own request. I'm too cowardly to be a cop, so this was the next best thing. I'm trying to suck up to the cops so they'll let me hang around." Sadie was thrilled by Jim's alliance.

"Oh, I love this. We will solve it together." Sadie had finally found a distraction. Now, it was a game. Try to figure out who wanted to kill Buddy…besides her.

"Sadie, do you really think a woman did it?"

"Of course, it's the only thing that makes sense. I don't have to play naïve with you, Jim, you know how much the Senator plays around."

Jim had the decency to look embarrassed, but wouldn't insult Sadie by pretending he didn't know.

"Do you have someone in mind, Sadie?"

"Too many to choose from, Jim. I don't know who his current chippy is, but that would be a place to start. At least you don't think it was me. I think most people do."

"I know it wasn't you, Sadie. I'll try to check around and see if I can find out what the Senator's been up to.

"Thanks for letting me interrupt. And, especially thanks for talking with me and giving me some ideas. You know you're one of my favorite people."

Sadie went weak in the knees. Jim always had that effect on her. He was so good looking, and so nice to her.

Sadie smiled good bye.

After expressing his pleasure with meeting Savannah, Jim turned to leave. Then, of course, Sadie suddenly became inappropriate.

"Oh, Jim, is there a reward for finding the would-be killer, or does the Senator have to die first?"

"Oh, Mama." Savannah shook her head and buried it in her hands.

Jim thought it was hilarious, because he thought she was kidding. After he left, Sadie got another reprimand from Savannah regarding—well, acting like—Sadie.

12

*W*hile Buddy was in intensive care, Sadie had let it be known she was in no mood to entertain anyone. She had Caroline spread the word that other than Savannah, a select few family members and Caroline—no one else would be welcomed with the usual ebullience of Sadie Montgomery.

"People pretty much need to leave me the fuck alone" were Sadie's exact words.

These words did not include her friend and neighbor, Bridgette O'Shay, but Sadie was still surprised when she looked up and saw Bridgette entering the ICU waiting room.

Checking out the beautifully dressed Bridgette, happily brought Sadie back to her shallow self. She felt her anxiety level lower and her shoulders lifted.

Sadie stood up to greet her. They hugged and Bridgette whispered, "I'm so sorry, Sadie."

"Thanks," Sadie responded as she led Bridgette to her private little corner in the waiting room.

Sadie gave Bridgette the once over. She was beautiful and rich. She had been a widow for twenty years. Sadie's first thought was "lucky broad" but then she remembered how much in love Bridgette and Joe had been. And he was so young. Bridgette had become something of a recluse since Joe's death. But Sadie was crazy about Bridgette in spite of that, and in spite of her great beauty and wealth. She was a good friend and neighbor—and very generous.

Minor problem: Bridgette kept her own counsel. She went about her business quietly. There was a great mystery about her. This came close to pissing Sadie off from time to time, because she didn't divulge her every move to Sadie. She even took trips without informing Sadie, every time.

Sadie was mostly pissed because of her own inability to keep her mouth shut about her personal business. She wanted to be mysterious. Fat chance!

Bridgette sat down beside Sadie and took her hand.

"Darling, what can I do for you? What an outrageous situation for you to find yourself in, and certainly not of your doing."

Sadie was immediately reminded that Bridgette was not a Southerner.

"Thank you, Bridgette, I'm getting through it. Wish I could be more gracious and cool. You know I aspire to be like you, but I fail miserably. I end up swearing and . . . Oh, Bridgette, you know how I am."

"You're darling, Sadie. I hope you realize that everyone is on your side in this nightmare you're living. No one pays any attention to those rude people who are making insinuations detrimental to your reputation."

Sadie loved the way Bridgette spoke. Without the Southern accent, she seemed more knowledgeable and authoritative. Or, was it her money? Lord Have Mercy! That woman was rich.

Sadie thanked her again. She wanted to hear much more about how great everyone thought she was, but being the lady

Bridgette was, she had stated her business and stood up to leave.

"Wait, Bridgette. Tell me how Susan is doing. I know you have been up there a couple of times. Is she okay?"

"She will be. We are discussing some possibilities for her. We'll go over all of it in detail when this is over and you're home. Then we can visit and I can get your input on some ideas. Thank you for asking."

She hugged Sadie again. "Darling, call me for anything. We'll have some fun when this is over. I miss your being next door. By the way, I hope you don't mind, I sent my landscape man over to do your yard. I asked him to add a couple of little surprises for you to enjoy just outside your sun room. I do hope you'll love them."

"Yeah, that kind of pisses me off, Bridgette. Loaning me the sapphire and diamond cuff was pretty rude, too.   You may have gone too far this time."

Bridgette laughed, gave her another hug, and sauntered out through the door.

She was so elegant. Sadie watched her leave. She could have easily hated her. If she weren't so nice, fun and rich.

Sadie felt better after Bridgette's visit. I must not be such a raging bitch if Bridgette likes me. Caroline was forced to be Sadie's friend, but Bridgette chose to be. Sadie reminded Caroline of that from time-to-time. Caroline would just shake her head and suggest Sadie grow up and stop being so insecure.

There! Even Caroline could be a bitch now and again.

13

$\mathcal{A}$ ritual had developed at the end of each and every day at the hospital. The doctor would come in to the Senator's room and give Sadie an up-date on his condition. He would inform her that Buddy was "slowly making progress."

At that point, she was dismissed to go back to the hotel to sleep.

What amazed Sadie was they "let" her go into Buddy's room twice a day for fifteen minutes at a time. They seemed to think they were doing her a favor. Sadie just sat by his bed, watching the clock. These fifteen minute torture times were the worst part of her day. She had nothing to say to Buddy. He was so drugged up, he barely acknowledged her and probably wouldn't understand what she said, so swearing at him was pointless. She took a book and managed to hide it from the nurses and doctors.

This went on for four days and nights. Each day he was more aware and showed annoyance when she left the room. It didn't matter, she didn't want to stay more than the allotted fifteen minutes, so she got out as soon as she could, ignoring his feeble protests.

Caroline had to go back to work, so she had deserted her. However, she came by every night and walked Sadie across the lawn to the hotel. She brought Sadie changes of clothing. Caroline knew it was vitally important to Sadie to look great at all times.

Savannah came by every day for a short time. She had the kids and her work.

Sadie missed the babies so much. Savannah would bring them sometimes and Sadie would go out and spend time with them.

Otherwise, these were some miserable days.

Jim Wilson came to visit with her often. She always enjoyed those visits. They made each other laugh.

Then one day, Jim brought a detective with him. The conversation turned more to questioning. Sadie answered all of them. She figured she was under suspicion in some way, but she didn't care. She was pretty sure she hadn't shot him, so she told them whatever they wanted to know.

In fact, she looked forward to these visits. If she was guilty, they sure found out how to get her to talk. She thought if she had shot him, what the hell! She might as well have the satisfaction of helping them figure it out.

Then, they started asking about her extramarital activities. Well, what the hell? Caroline wasn't there to stop her, so Sadie bragged away. She left nothing out. This was really entertaining for her. She rarely got to go on and on about her affairs.

Sadly, they soon lost interest and went back to questions regarding her husband's escapades. Well, that was boring as hell, but better than sitting and staring into space. They even brought in a second detective. Apparently, they were serious about finding a suspect.

Sadie knew a lot about what her husband did and with whom, but not all of it, of course. Sadie did the best she could to provide them with everything she knew, but she had to admit, there was much more she didn't know.

There were so many possibilities. Not only the women, but their angry men friends or husbands. Sadie couldn't possibly know all about them, nor did she really want to waste her time with it. Never mind all the people who held him responsible for their discontent with certain of his political beliefs and positions.

They were questioning all of the Senator's staff. It would take them years to track everyone down who would want to do the bastard harm, Sadie thought to herself. Would they never lose interest in this? Who cares who shot him? Didn't everyone who knew him want to?

The fact that she was able to keep these thoughts to herself made her proud. She hadn't needed the prompting of Caroline or Savannah. Hah!

14

*A*bout the fifth day of Buddy's hospitalization, Sadie was attempting to devise a way out of this new and different incarceration. The only reason they were keeping Buddy now was because he was still weak and it was a way to protect him from whoever wanted him dead. Didn't they know how foolish it was to allow Sadie to visit him? Never mind.

That evening, when Caroline arrived to bring another set of clothes, Sadie's mood was black. As Caroline walked Sadie across the hospital lawn to her hotel room, Sadie informed Caroline she was sick of this and wanted to go back to a normal existence.

"Since when do you call your regular life normal?" Caroline was attempting to bring Sadie out of her black mood.

"No, I don't have a normal life, but I did have some semblance of freedom. You know I can put on a show, give an award-winning performance when it comes to pretending to be almost sane. But I've met my limit. My public persona is no longer that important to me."

"Good Lord, Sadie. Do you hear what you're saying? Don't stroke out on me now, girl. I'm getting almost as much publicity out of this as you are. Do you know they photograph me coming into the hospital bringing your change of clothes?

I'm on television every day. Don't deny me this small bit of notoriety. The doctor told you tonight Buddy was going to be fine. He's talking more and he's sitting up all the time and walking around some, he'll be out of here in no time."

"Are you trying to help me, Caroline or depress me?" Sadie refused to let go of the stubbornness.

"It's almost over, Sadie. Just another day. Two at the most and he'll get to go home."

Sadie was silent. This concerned Caroline. They put Sadie's clothes away and gathered up the ones for Caroline to take back, all in total silence.

Caroline hugged Sadie. "I promise you, he will be dismissed and you will get to go back to your house in a couple of days, tomorrow or the next day. I promise."

"Caroline, you have never pretended to have psychic abilities before. I find this disturbing. I'll walk you outside, but please show some dignity. Being raised a snake-handler, I'm embarrassed for you."

The two friends giggled like high school girls as they walked outside. Sadie walked with Caroline to the parking lot and to her car. Just as they had done for the last several nights.

A couple of reporters were yelling questions and photographers were filming them. The security guards had ordered them back and Sadie and Caroline ignored them.

Out of the corner of her eye, Sadie took notice of two of the detectives and a uniformed policeman standing outside the emergency room, letting the security men take care of the press and watching Sadie and Caroline. They were talking and smoking. She longed to join them. She so hated her lack of innocent conversation and flirtation.

She kissed her oldest friend on the cheek and thanked her for being there for her. Then, Sadie turned and started back toward her room.

Suddenly, she heard a woman yell.

"You bitch!"

Sadie turned and looked up toward the shrill voice, then she heard a loud crack and simultaneously felt a searing, burning pain in her entire upper body. Sadie screamed as loud as she could before everything went black.

Caroline was getting in her car when she heard the yell, the shot and the scream.

The detectives and the uniformed officer had all been watching Sadie surreptitiously.

Everyone froze for about three seconds before they realized what they were seeing and hearing. Then, everyone was in full motion.

Caroline was the first to run to Sadie. The detectives and police officer started running to her. They saw a women jump into a dark, late model Ford Explorer, and speed away. The policeman called in the information on the Explorer. One detective called the emergency room, so, by the time they reached Sadie on the ground, paramedics were running out the doors with a gurney.

Sadie's torso was soaked in blood. "Oh God," someone whispered as they knelt down, closer to Sadie. Caroline was screaming, crying and trying to feel Sadie's carotid artery for a pulse.

Caroline heard someone say, "Maybe she was the target from the beginning?" Then she started screaming louder.

The paramedics loaded Sadie onto the gurney. One was stripping away Sadie's blouse as they ran the few yards to the emergency room.

One detective, studying the ground where Sadie had lain, yelled for someone to get him more light. "I need to find that bullet."

At that point, Caroline stumbled.

"Jeeze." One of the officers mumbled as he caught her just before she hit the ground.

Another officer appeared at the site where the long-gone Explorer had been parked. "I've got the casing," he yelled and ran with his flashlight to the detective searching for the bullet. Nothing there and no one had been able to identify any part of the license plate.

Sadie was unconscious and losing a great deal of blood.

The photographers were in full mode from the minute Sadie had fallen and everyone realized what had happened. No one was stopping them, other than keeping them out of the way of the paramedics and the gurney. Sadie's exposure as she lay limp on the gurney being carried to the emergency entrance, would be fully documented on film and it would soon be on television for all to see.

15

*S*ally carefully aimed the gun at Sadie's heart, screaming "You Bitch!" She pulled the trigger and hesitated just long enough to watch Sadie Montgomery fall to the ground. Then she scrambled into her SUV, frantically heading out of the parking lot, tires squealing. She was laughing as she drove wildly, taking the back streets to her home.

Her heart was pounding out of her chest and her breath came in spasms. She'd done it! She'd killed the miserable bitch who'd made her life a living hell for years. Sally would be the last person to come under suspicion. Mousy little Sally Blevins. She knew what people said about her behind her back. Dull, unimaginative, always trying too hard. Sadie said it just by the looks she gave Sally.

Maybe Sally could never be glamorous and life of the party as 'so in love with herself' Sadie Montgomery. Well, guess who finally won the battle? The Mouse herself.

She would have the Senator to herself, Sally would be the one strolling around on Buddy's arm. Queen Bee Sadie always seemed to float in front of everyone, waiting for them to fall to their knees in adoration. Well, now Sadie was dead, gone and soon to be forgotten.

Even Buddy didn't think Sally had the nerve to do this. Since their affair started years ago and Sadie had caught them, Buddy had kept her in the shadows and dark alleys. It was absolutely necessary to protect dear Sadie. So Sally did everything Buddy asked.

Finally, it was going to pay off. Buddy would be her devoted husband.

She was shaking so she almost fell out of her Explorer. She remembered to remove the scarf she had pinned over the license plate.

Sally still felt her heart would explode. She needed to keep reminding herself that all this was necessary to clear the way for her to become the new Mrs. Buddy Montgomery. She'd finally have the respect she deserved.

She closed the garage door, shutting away her navy blue Explorer.

Somehow, after much fumbling, she managed to unlock her front door. She was safely inside. No one had seen her, no one could see her now and no one knew. Buddy would protect her. He would have to—to reward her bravery for being the one to clear the way for their future together.

Unlike Sadie, she would be good to Buddy. She would never treat him so casually as Sadie had. She hated the way Buddy fawned over Sadie in public. He said it was something he had to do for his reputation to show everyone he had a good, loving marriage. Of course he wasn't in love with Sadie! Sally should know better than that.

She needed to put all that away out of her head. Everything was changed now. Thanks to the former mouse, Sally Blevins. She had almost ruined everything when the first bullet meant for Sadie had hit Buddy. God! She felt sick just thinking about it. But she would be able to explain to Buddy that that first bullet at the Capitol had hit him only because when she was finally able to get off her shot, suddenly Sadie had jerked away and Buddy's head was where Sadie's had been. But it was too late. Sally had thought she had killed Buddy and had gone running and screaming to her car. She had gone to her house fully intending to kill herself if Buddy had died.

Thank goodness he was all right and Sally would be able to explain to him. Buddy would understand and be so proud of her that she didn't coward out after that mishap. She had pulled herself together and gone after her real target, and by God this time she had nailed her.

She decided to shower, washing away the ugly past.

She went into the bathroom, fully clothed and carrying her purse. She undressed and got into the hot shower, feeling all the anxiety drift away.

She smiled as she dried off. She reached into her purse and took out the gun. She was preening and posing in front of the mirror, using the gun as a prop. She posed, Charlie's Angels style, looking all sexy and dangerous. That gun had set them free. She and Buddy.

As she looked in the mirror, she realized she had become absolutely beautiful. It was Sadie's arrogance that had caused Sally to appear insecure. Sadie had made her look bad. Sadie, with her long, shapely legs, which she managed to show off all the time. Couldn't Buddy see what a slut Sadie was?

But no more! There would be no more snubbing of Sally Blevins Montgomery.

Buddy would get out of the hospital soon. Of course there would have to be a funeral for Sadie. More of Buddy's acting devoted, but then a few weeks would go by and they could be together publicly. All their plans falling neatly into place.

She finished drying off and not bothering with a robe, she went directly to the kitchen for a bottle of wine. She popped some popcorn and carried her goodies to the sofa.

Excitedly, she turned on the television. There had been plenty of time for the news of Sadie Montgomery's death to be announced.

Yes! There it was! Big time activity outside the hospital. Policemen running hither and yon. 'No comments' coming from the hospital staff.

Oh, and there was Sadie being loaded onto a gurney. She was covered in blood. Whoopie! What a sight! There was a close-up on Sadie's face, eyes closed, looking all helpless and dead. Beautiful in death. People would soon forget her and her loveliness. A lot of good it did you bitch!

Oh my God! This was thrilling. Sally sat cross-legged on the sofa, gulping her wine, chomping on her popcorn. She couldn't stop giggling. Buddy should be calling as soon as he could manage some privacy.

He would generously reward her for stepping up and making it possible for them to have the glamorous life he had promised her.

True, he had been slow coming to a decision. He almost seemed afraid of Sadie. So were a lot of people. Well, whatever! Sadie's hold on him was gone now. Sally would never again have to see Sadie strolling across the room with Buddy trailing behind his Queen Sadie. He had assured Sally it was just one more thing he had to do to keep up the front as a happy couple.

Sally opened another bottle of wine. Put the bitch out of your mind! He belongs to Sally Blevins now. And, let's face it,

Sally now had quite the hammer to hold over Buddy's head. She had set him free. He would owe her.

"Sadie Montgomery's condition is still unknown at this time."

What the fuck! Not known! She's dead! Say she's dead!

"... rumors are whirling around that Mrs. Montgomery has died. But remember these are just rumors. We have had no official word. Once again, we cannot confirm Sadie Montgomery's condition. We can only tell you she had been shot by an unknown assailant and is in grave condition inside this very hospital where her husband, Senator Buddy Montgomery is also a patient. He, too, is suffering from a gun shot wound, but as we know, is recovering nicely. We will give you the latest on Sadie Montgomery's condition as soon as we can get an update."

Sally laughed and gulped down the rest of that glass of wine. She poured another.

"That's more like it!" She said aloud as she settled in to wait for the good news.

But the 'on again, off again—she's dead, she's not dead, she may be dead' was grating on her nerves. Good God! How long was this going to go on?

Sadie was at death's door, if not dead. Sally was an excellent shot. She knew that bullet had penetrated Sadie's cold, hard heart. What was the hold up? No matter. Sally knew Sadie was gone, gone, gone.

She'd hear from Buddy soon. Of course that's why they aren't announcing Sadie's death. They would have to inform Buddy of her death before they made a formal announcement on television.

Sally finished off that bottle and opened another. She was pretty drunk now and impatient that there had been no announcement and she hadn't heard from Buddy.

She threw a handful of popcorn at this television, cursing it and everyone on it.

She got really brave and called Buddy's room at the hospital. No answer. She let it ring until it rolled over to the nurses station. Sally was slurring her words and incoherent. The nurse finally hung up on her.

" . . . waiting here as Sadie Montgomery's life hangs in the balance."

Okay! Good enough! Sally poured another glass of wine, spilling it all over the coffee table and its contents. She'd just wait for her to die. Don't know why the hell it was taking so long. Screw it. She had nothing but time. She'd just lay down on the sofa and catch a nap and when she woke up, Sadie's death would be confirmed and Sally's new life would begin.

16

*T*otal chaos ensued and enveloped the emergency room. Caroline was the first to be ordered out of the emergency room.

She stumbled out into the waiting room. David, who had been in Buddy's room, was running up the hall in an attempt to discover the cause of all the commotion.

Caroline saw Dr. McKenzie, Sadie's personal physician, running into the E.R. That sight gave her some sense of relief.

The detectives and other officers were next to be ousted from the emergency room.

Caroline was waiting for them. "Please, just tell me she's alive. Tell me she's okay! Please!"

The last of the detectives to walk out of the emergency room announced, "I know she's alive and losing a lot of blood. They said she had gone into shock from it. I didn't find the bullet that hit her. Were you close enough to recognize the women who shot her?" He asked Caroline.

"No!" Caroline sobbed. "She was between another car and the one she drove off in. Did anyone get a license plate number?"

"Son-of-a-bitch. No." She heard one of the officers mumble in frustration.

"We're pretty sure there was something on the plate to prevent any identification. The color was navy, or maybe black. Seemed more blue, though. Still not impossible to find." He was trying desperately to come up with something positive. How could this have happened right under their noses?

The emergency room doors opened and out they came, wheeling a gurney with Sadie on it. She had tubes coming out everywhere.

"What's wrong? Where are you taking her?" Caroline demanded of anyone and everyone.

"She's going to surgery. We have to do some tying off to stop the bleeding and the x-rays show the bullet missed the lung, cracked a rib, but it's lodged close to her heart. We've got to get it out." Dr. McKenzie told Caroline.

"What am I supposed to tell her daughter?" Caroline asked him.

"Tell Savannah to get up here. Now."

"Oh God, oh God . . . ." It was the only response Caroline could manage.

A policeman was accompanying Sadie's gurney up to surgery. They weren't letting anyone near her.

Caroline and David stood together as they watched the gurney being maneuvered onto the elevator. Caroline turned to David, "I have to go get Savannah. Dr. McKenzie said to."

"Shit. I was trying to forget that part." David responded. It was yet to be seen exactly how successful the two were going to be in carrying out these instructions together. They were still too much in shock themselves.

They were interrupted by a nurse coming from the I.C.U., they knew only from her badge. "The Senator is feeling much better and he is insisting his wife be brought to him immediately." The nurse was beaming as though she was bringing news of world peace. Obviously, she hadn't heard of the latest catastrophe.

When no one responded to her, the nurse repeated. "The Senator wants to see his wife before he goes to sleep. He would like to have her brought to him now."

David said simply, "Sadie's not available." He took Caroline's arm, urging her forward, towards the elevators. Leaving the nurse with her mouth hanging open.

"What a royal fuck-up." David was shaking his head as he led Caroline onto an elevator where they couldn't be heard. "No one got a license plate number. No one can identify the shooter, other than the voice being female. What the hell are we going to do?"

Caroline was sobbing softly now. "Dr. McKenzie said we need to get Savannah up here."

"I'll go with you, you shouldn't go by yourself, and I'm not entirely sure we shouldn't take an officer with us." They were now standing outside the Operating Room.

"I've got to call my husband." Caroline said.

David flagged down a nearby detective he recognized. Caroline watched as David talked to the detective. She didn't get an answer from Wagner, but, truth be known, she wasn't sure she had even dialed the correct number.

"We need to go now." David said as he and the detective each took one of Caroline's arms and headed outside to a car.

Inside, the confused and somewhat offended I.C.U. nurse, had finally discovered what had happened to Sadie. No way was she going to be the one to tell the Senator. She decided to tell the Senator's doctor and let him handle it.

Caroline, David and the detective drove to Savannah's house. The short trip was quiet and uncomfortable. Each lost in their own thoughts.

They got out of the car and went up to the door together. Beau answered. He quickly assessed the situation, "Oh, no! What's wrong? My God, has Buddy died?"

Caroline stepped up and grabbed Beau, hugging him as much as she was using him for physical stability. She was pretty sure she could faint at any moment. Just the thought of having to tell Savannah what had happened made her woozy.

"Beau, something horrible has happened, but it's not Buddy. It's Sadie."

Beau stepped outside and immediately, but quietly, closed the door. He knew well enough that he needed to be prepared before his wife heard any of this.

"Oh shit! What happened? What is it, Caroline?" He was beginning to panic.

"She's in surgery, Beau. It's too soon to know how she's going to come out of this.

"Beau, someone shot her." She started sobbing again. Beau held her, but he began shaking too.

Beau looked at David and the detective. Quite frankly, he was hoping one of them was going to volunteer to tell his wife that her mother had been shot and was in surgery. Her condition uncertain. No volunteers.

Beau pulled Caroline away, but didn't let go of her. The only reassurance he was feeling was that he had managed to calm her somewhat.

"Jesus Caroline, I can't tell Savannah. God, what a nightmare!" He took one more look at the people on his porch. Damn! Still no volunteers.

"Shit." He said as he opened the door to the house with one hand, and held tightly to Caroline's hand with his other.

Savannah walked into the foyer just as Beau led the small crowd into the house. She was dressed in a tee shirt, sans bra, and her favorite pair of jeans. She had been at her computer, writing.

The entourage just stood there, looking at her.

Beau, much to the others' relief, was the first to get it together and he instinctively went to his wife and took her in his arms.

"Oh no! It's Buddy, he's dead!" Tears were already flowing down Savannah's face.

"Baby, it's not Buddy." Beau said cautiously.

Savannah pushed Beau away. "What is it, Beau. Tell me. What?!"

"Your mother. Baby, I'm sorry. She's alive, but . . . she's been shot."

"Ohhh." Savannah's eyes rolled back and Beau felt her start to crumble. His legs weren't so stable either, so, as she slid to her knees, he sank to the floor along with her, holding tightly to his wife.

Caroline grabbed for both of them. The pile of bodies that accumulated on the floor was anything but attractive.

David and the detective just shuffled their feet, feeling useless and out of place. They would rather be anywhere but here.

It was a sobbing Caroline that brought Savannah back to reality.

Savannah opened her eyes, looked at Beau seeing the tears running down his face. She let out a blood-curdling scream (not unlike the one the detective had heard Sadie emit earlier).

Savannah's scream turned into an odd, animal-like wail and she collapsed in tears.

"My god. Let's get her to the hospital." The detective said as David had already braved the pile to help Beau peel Caroline and Savannah off the floor.

Beau wouldn't let go of Savannah. He asked Caroline to dial his parents' home. She held the phone to Beau's ear and mouth, the phone shaking with Caroline's hand. It was difficult, but he managed to relay these latest hideous bits of news to his father. Beau wasn't processing much and not really able to follow much of what came out on the other end of the line, as Caroline tried her best to hold the phone steady, but he felt it safe to assume they were on their way.

As Beau helped Savannah up, he asked David to go next door. Beau and Savannah were very close to their neighbors and Beau instructed David to ask one of them to come over immediately to stay with the kids until his parents could get to the house. Hopefully the children were still sleeping, Savannah's scream had been a doozy.

Savannah was crying and saying over and over again "Oh no, oh no". Beau, Caroline, David and the detective started moving her toward the car. Beau passed his neighbor on the way, thanking her and telling her his folks would be there soon. She just nodded and let them go, signs of a good friend.

David turned to Beau. "Give me your keys. I'll bring your car to the hospital."

"Thanks." Beau said as he blindly handed the keys to David. Then he loaded Caroline and Savannah, who were holding tightly to each other, into the unmarked police car.

Savannah was trying to calm herself but everything she said was through hysterical tears. She was unable to hear, or comprehend the answers to any of the questions she was asking, so she continued to ask them over and over.

The nightmare journey to the hospital finally ended. The four stumbled out of the police car and David pulled in beside them.

They headed for the emergency room.

David and the detective ran ahead to get the information before it was relayed to Savannah.

The news wasn't great. Sadie was unconscious but already out of surgery. Her vital signs were good. Many little arteries, etc., had to be repaired to stop the bleeding. They were able to locate and retrieve the bullet. She had lost a lot of blood and had gone into shock, but the surgery was over quickly and they were getting ready to move her to I.C.U.

The news of Buddy's having been moved out of I.C.U. was anticlimactic.

Upon hearing of Sadie's injury, Buddy made a huge fuss. He insisted on Sadie being put in his room.

"Out of the question!" was the loud response from everyone.

Buddy was causing quite a scene, but about four people had been sent to his room to be sure he remained calm and quiet. The injection was the only thing that shut him up.

Savannah was allowed to go in with Sadie. Savannah had never seen her mother unconscious, so completely helpless. She held her mother's hand, stroked her hair and kissed her forehead. Try as she might, she was still sobbing uncontrollably.

Dr. McKenzie came in and offered Savannah an injection to calm her down. She took it. Mother/daughter common belief in better living through chemistry. Caroline got them to move a bed into Sadie's room in I.C.U., for Savannah.

This had impressed the entourage that had become Sadie's over the last hours, as this was far from common practice. But Caroline knew Savannah's presence would bring Sadie back quicker than anything. She also planned to keep the Senator as far from Sadie as possible. She corralled David and the detective to keep the "demanding jackass away from Sadie through whatever means necessary."

Beau began to relax once he saw Caroline regain control and take charge. He was then able to insist Caroline be driven home. Her clothes were pretty muddled—a great deal of Sadie's blood was on her blouse. She was ready to collapse. So when she was assured all her requests had been followed, she allowed David to take her home in her car while one of the uniformed officers followed in a squad car to bring David directly back to the hospital.

Now, there was nothing left for Beau, David and the detectives to do except wander the halls and speculate on what the hell had happened.

News people from the paper and television had swarmed the hospital. Someone had been dispatched to give them a statement, and to keep them in a confined area, away from the family.

Jim Wilson was given the exclusive because of his, by now, well-known friendship with Sadie.

Beau's father soon arrived at the hospital, too. He had left his wife to care for the children. He knew he needed to be with Beau and Savannah. And he had clout of his own to use to ensure that his family was protected from the media, or anyone else for that matter.

Beau felt like he was in an ongoing nightmare. They let him go to the door of the I.C.U. to see Savannah sleeping peacefully on a cot next to her unconscious mother. The tears flowed heavily again as he watched them.

The news had traveled quickly about a woman in an Explorer shooting Sadie Montgomery.

Oh, the speculation. Had Sadie been messing around with someone's husband? Boyfriend?

Actually, no one knew of any messing around Sadie had done for years. Caroline, who had been unable to stay away from the hospital and had insisted Wagner take her right back once she changed clothes and freshened up a bit, was the closest to Sadie, and she assured them Sadie had been nothing but a proper wife. How dare they suggest otherwise.

Caroline had slowly taken over Sadie's suite at the hospital hotel. Using it only to shower, change her clothes and immediately return to the I.C.U. waiting room. Now it was Lucy bringing her changes of clothes and making her eat.

Mid-morning the day after the shooting, Savannah awoke. The screaming started shortly after and the second sedation followed shortly after that. Beau tried to relay the story of the shooting as he understood it while Savannah was calm, but she was accepting none of it.

Caroline knew how bad things were with Sadie when Savannah's screams didn't awaken her.

The Senator was furious that he was allowed only to look in the window at Sadie a couple of times a day. Everyone was his enemy, or so it seemed. Sadie's doctor, Dr. McKenzie had complete control over her care and Buddy had no pull with him.

Buddy demanded his own doctor, Dr. Rush, get him answers. He wouldn't accept that there were no answers to give at that point. Thus, Dr. Rush decided it would be best if he ordered an increase in Buddy's pain meds. Even he'd had enough when the Senator continued to threaten the hospital staff if his wife wasn't "brought to him immediately."

Sadie's vitals were improving and she showed signs of waking, especially when Savannah was touching her or talking to her.

Caroline was successful in getting Savannah to go to Sadie's hotel room and shower.

Beau brought her clean clothes and was spending as much time at the hospital as he could. He didn't want the kids to worry any more than they already were.

The next night Savannah had to leave the hospital and go home. She was emotionally and physically exhausted.

On the drive home she began to cry softly, again. She might not have her mother another day.

This can't happen. Sadie's a strong woman. She'd been through so damned much, she could pull through this.

Savannah tried to put it out of her mind and think about Beau and the kids.

When she arrived home, they were all sound asleep. She suspected Beau had played hard with them to exhaust them into sleep.

She went to the old family trunk where their favorite things and ancestral treasures were kept. She wanted to find the original baby quilts Sadie had handmade for Roger Montgomery and Catie Vee, when they were first born. She took the little quilts, each somewhat worn, but still beautiful, to their beds and tucked Catie Vee's quilt up around her, and kissed her pretty little face. Then she went to Roger Montgomery's room. She was tucking the quilt up around him, when he drowsily reached for Savannah and hugged her. Then he took the quilt and said "Thank you, Mama. I love you." He turned over and hugged the quilt to him. Savannah kissed him goodnight and went back to close the trunk. She noticed an envelope that had been under the quilts.

She picked it up and realized it was a crazy, funny story Sadie had written within hours after Savannah had told her she was engaged to marry Beau.

Savannah had been so over-the-top happy and giddy. She had told Sadie, "Start planning. Make some notes of ideas. Get this thing going."

Sadie had rolled her eyes, then spiked an eyebrow. "Yeah, Buttons, I'll get right on that."

Savannah had dropped back by the house a couple of hours later to get a bridal magazine she had forgotten.

When she was leaving, Sadie said "By the way, Toots, here's my ideas for your wedding. Enjoy!"

Savannah had grabbed the envelope and hadn't read it until she got back to her house. On this now yellowing paper was what Sadie had written for her.

Article From The Crow Mountain Gazette (Society Page)

Talk of the Town:

Wedding of prominent citizen, the lovely Savannah Davis, and the (as of this writing) never seen by any of Crow Mountain's town folk, and known only as 'Elden the Weird'.

Ms. Jules Wilson, the Social Savvy Lady of our area, has contacted us with additional plans regarding the wedding of the decade. Ms. Wilson's nose kept twitching as though she were smelling something very unpleasant as she relayed the details.

Two well-known local ladies have become the latest additions to a spectacle which is destined to become the most talked about wedding the Skyline Mobile Home

Trailer Park has seen. The inclusion of Gabby Layton and Sarah Cameron in the fiasco, has caused quite a stir amongst the town folk. These two popular ladies are known in the "beer and sawdust" crowd as a couple of "good old gals who would liven up any 'throw-down'."

Grace Ann Martin will be featured as flower girl and Tamara Prince will accompany her down the aisle as ring bearer. They will be leaping and skipping down the aisle singing "Stand by Your Man". This rendition of a time-honored ditty will be sung *a capella*, as these lovelies need absolutely no accompaniment and would not likely receive help from anyone, anyway. We want to apologize for last year's Country Barbecue, when the two were asked to sing a capella and they performed a striptease, not knowing what the word meant. We promise you this will not happen again, at least by Grace Ann Martin, who's display caused three young boys and a clergyman to be admitted to the nervous hospital, where they remain to this day. It is also questionable as to whether Grace Ann will be able to leap or skip (waddle, perhaps).

Further instructions regarding arrival at the bowling alley for the nuptials have been issued. Each guest will be rubbed down with a mixture of coal-oil, linseed oil and diesel fuel (they wish me to explain this is strictly for health purposes due to the pungency of floral accents— with which Grace Ann Martin's delicate lungs cannot contend), but also to ward off insects. As those of us who have lived in this exclusive motor home park have become accustomed, we don't expect any complaints. A vat of this elixir will be available outside the bowling alley immediately preceding the ceremony for those wishing to join in the festivities, but have delicate skin. It has been witnessed and reported to this newspaper reporter, that Sara Cameron and a drifter who had the misfortune of being caught under the spell of the seductive chippy, had been seen at the last throw-down the bowling alley sponsored, swigging down this medicinal concoction (meant only for topical application), when the home-made beer and white lightnin' ran out. We pray regularly for this unfortunate drifter. Sadly he is still serving time in the State Penitentiary and will not come up for parole until the year 2019. It makes no matter to him, as he has lost all memory and has no idea who he is, where he came from or who his people are.

The charming Grace Ann Martin and Sarah Cameron will arrive at the church on a flat-bed truck decorated with hollyhocks, honeysuckle and Black-eyed Susans. They will carry stalks of Hydrangea blossoms and red Canna. They will be resplendent in ruffled creations of purple taffeta and red taffeta (as I pen this, slapping and hair-pulling are taking place in the background in an attempt to decide who will wear which color. Their individual tastes and combined flair for the exotic will probably lead to a combination of each). They will be wearing color-coordinated decorative hosiery, topped off with white patent leather mules, with live goldfish swimming in water in the 3-inch heels. (I've heard Ms. Sarah wears a size 11 and ½ Double Wide—but this may be a product of the vicious tongue of Grace Anne at work again. There is rumored to be some jealousy between these fun-lovin' cuties).

As this newspaper prepares to go to press, a sad and grotesque story has come to light. Grace Anne's unfortunate weight gain (some say she is galloping rapidly toward 250 pounds) has caused her three-inch heels to collapse. Now we have some young children who have witnessed the power-pressured, crushing death of the poor goldfish. The young children will, no doubt, suffer emotional consequences for a very long time.

Ms. Martin has been rushed to the Gloryland Hospital Emergency Room and the medical personnel have been unable to sedate her. Her many years of drug use and abuse have rendered the usual medications ineffective.

Word has it, the ambulance driver (Mr. Skinner who owns and operates the hog farm just down the road) has been ordered to "drive like a bat out of hell" to get to the zoo and get a bucket of elephant tranquilizers. There will continue to be a SWAT team outside the Gloryland Hospital until Mr. Skinner returns with the much needed sedation. We beg all citizens to stay away from the hospital as Ms. Martin's behavior has always been unpredictable.

However this turns out, sadly, this will be Ms. Grace's final public performance. She is being retired (put out to pasture) due to her advancing age and many physical and mental infirmities. (Her 80 pound weight gain 'has nothing to do with her retirement,' Ms. Martin spat at this reporter.) However, Ms. Wilson seemed somewhat relieved to pass this news along.

The always secretive Ms. Davis refuses to give out any information regarding her hubby-to-be. She just smiles while her eyes and feet dance with anticipation. She promises that even though this will be her ninth marriage, it will still hold some shocking surprises and thrills. Ms. Wilson said she has no public comment to make on the subject.

Carlene Maggots, as we all know, works in the finer fabrics department of Wal-Mart, has been selected to design and make the wedding frock for Ms. Davis. Our sources inform us that Carlene has been seen sewing sparkling, multi-colored sequins onto a brilliant metallic orange fabric. "You can't prove this is part of her dress," screeched Carlene when approached by this reporter. However, pale lavender patent leather sling-back stiletto heels have been special-ordered by the Wal-Mart shoe department. Sounds like the perfect blend of colors—something for which Ms. Davis is well-known.

This mysterious groom will also be wearing, as part of his formal attire, the silver lame spandex pedal pushers. This has been a staple in all of Ms. Davis' weddings. She remarked to us that she would never marry a man that couldn't carry off this truth-telling garment. So far all of her grooms have done the pedal pushers proud. She thinks this one will be the most impressive thus far and doesn't want any of the ladies of the county to miss out on this eye-full.

Ms. Wilson, clad as usual in a gold silk belly-dancers' outfit and the well-known and well-worn gold silk turban, appeared horrified that this bit of information had leaked out. She seemed to be in quite a snit as she left, muttering about this very well may be the last wedding she plans and reports for Ms. Davis. As no matter what a hefty sum Ms. Davis pays her, the humiliation was becoming too much. Well, we all know Ms. Jules Wilson better than that, don't we?

Late Update:

Two women, each being described as "raving maniacs" have come flying into town, each claiming to be the mother of the very odd groom.

This reporter's research has uncovered documents verifying that these two women were, at one time, popular table dancers in Mexico.

The blonde hussy, who is known in the exotic dancers' circle as "Cat" does seem to have some legal documents which may prove her claim.

No member of the bride's family can be located.

Savannah re-read this ridiculous little story, laughing and crying. Sadie has to be okay. Savannah needed this crazy woman around her. She sat there for a few more minutes, then put the writing back into the trunk.

She crawled into bed and snuggled up to Beau, trying to will her mother to be awake and better tomorrow.

17

After Savannah had been forced to go to her home to rest and be with her children, Caroline settled in for the long haul. If Savannah was gone, there was no way Caroline would leave Sadie.

Caroline and Sadie had been close for years—since their daughters were about five. No one knew them better than each other.

Sadie was someone Caroline could always confide in, and she knew Sadie would always have her back. Caroline constantly proved her loyalty to Sadie. Sadie trusted no one as much as she trusted Caroline.

Caroline got a little light headed when she thought of life without Sadie.

Sadie regularly thought up the most wonderful, wild and fun things for the two of them and Lucy and Savannah to do. Neither Sadie nor Caroline had had good childhoods. Their families had been dirt poor. They wanted their girls raised in a larger town that offered more opportunities.

A couple of years after they met, Sadie was offered an opportunity for Savannah to attend a horse ranch for a week, including riding classes and at the end of the week, a girl's attire contest and a contest for original decoration of each girl's assigned horse. Sadie found a way for Lucy to attend the camp with Savannah and made arrangements for she and Caroline to drive the girls the one hundred miles to the camp, visit them mid-week and go up for the last day's activities.

That was just an example of Sadie's generosity. Caroline knew that many people's perception of Sadie was of a shallow, self-centered woman. But that changed when they got to know her, even though Sadie appeared to promote these misconceptions of herself. Very few people disliked her. If they did, it involved jealousy. Sadie was well read, bright and introspective and caring.

Caroline remembered the first day she met Sadie. Sadie was the new woman at work and causing quite a stir. Sadie was shy and nervous and tried to hide it by acting aloof. Caroline saw right through Sadie's snooty facade.

It turned out, Sadie and Caroline lived within a block of each other. Sadie was divorced and professed to be sick of men. Despite this, Sadie and Wagner got along well, constantly teasing and bickering.

There was a negative side to Sadie. One that tried Caroline's patience on many occasions. Sadie could go into deep depressions and withdraw from everyone. Almost as disturbing as this was her miserable choice of men. She had many to choose from, and sadly, always chose the manipulative bastard she should run from.

Caroline had been against the marriage to Buddy, but there was no reasoning with Sadie. Sadie's Aunt Jaqleen and Caroline had done everything but threaten to have her locked up. They finally had to play tick-a-lock to keep their close relationships intact.

Caroline sat softly crying at her memories when she felt someone sit down next to her. She looked up to see Wagner, her decent, devoted husband as he enveloped her in his arms. She let herself go and sobbed quietly into Wagner's shoulder.

18

On the third day of Sadie's hospital stay, Savannah was sitting on her mother's bed, talking to her. Sadie's eyes fluttered and she reached for Savannah's hand. The doctor was called and the nurses rushed in.

There wasn't much more out of Sadie until the fourth day. Again, Savannah was holding her hand and talking to her.

Sadie opened her eyes and looked up at Savannah and asked, "Why the fuck would Sally Blevins want to shoot me?" Then Sadie faded out again. Savannah was curious, but assumed it was the medication talking. She was so glad her mother was showing signs of improvement.

The next time she woke up was about an hour later. She came to in full force.

"Stupid-assed bitch! Tried to kill me!"

Savannah jerked awake. She had been sitting by her mother's bed in the Intensive Care Unit. She hadn't been given much encouragement by the doctors.

"We'll have to wait and see. She's lost a lot of blood, but her vitals are good. Unless something unforeseen happens, we expect a full recovery, but it may be slow.

Savannah should have known better, as Sadie came to with a vengeance.

"The bitch tried to kill me. She better be behind bars. And they need to keep a guard at my door. She probably didn't act alone.

"Savannah, my baby. I'm so glad to see you. Look how pretty you are. Thank you for being here, my pretty little girl." Out again. She wasted her energy very quickly.

Word went out to the detectives, agents, David, Caroline—everyone—even the Senator.

They let one detective come in to question Sadie only for a short time and only when Savannah was with her.

What did Sadie see? Hear? Sadie was very clear about what had happened.

"I was watching Caroline leave and I heard Sally Blevins yell, 'you bitch'. I looked up at her standing by her navy Explorer and saw her raise a gun. God! My chest hurt like hell. I guess I fainted. I don't remember anything else 'til . . . here I am.

"What do you suppose I did to piss her off? I haven't seen her in a year. Who would have thought the little mouse owned a gun, or could use one! What the hell? I could have been killed. Remind me to get back at that miserable little mouse. She upset my poor Savannah.

"And send flowers to whoever is keeping Buddy away from me." Sadie had fallen back asleep. She slept a lot. They said she had to, the sleep would help her recovery.

The next morning, Savannah was sitting on Sadie's bed, pushing her hair off her face and just looking at her. How close she had come to losing her Mama.

Sadie opened her eyes. She and Savannah looked at each other, both their eyes filling with tears.

"Savannah, sweetheart."

"What, Mama?"

"I'm so glad it wasn't you who tried to kill me. I wouldn't have ratted you out, you know. I'm a very devoted and loyal mother."

Savannah looked at her mother and, before she could totally process Sadie's joke, her mother rolled her eyes.

"Oh, Jesus Christ, Mama. Keep that shit up and next time it will be me. Let it go, will ya? I wouldn't have told anyone even if you had managed to kill Buddy with such a feeble attempt as that." Savannah gave her mother a sly smile.

"Now that's my girl." Sadie said proudly. "I knew you had it in ya." They were laughing now and hugging each other.

"I love you so much, Mama."

"I love you too, Buttons. You're the best kid I ever had. Don't you believe what other people have told you I said."

More giggles, then they were interrupted by a jovial nurse announcing, "You're doing so well, Mrs. Montgomery, your husband is insisting you be wheeled down to his room. Right now! Isn't that great?"

Sadie suddenly became demon-possessed. She hissed at the nurse.

"Your job is not to come in here and tell me when I have to see Senator Montgomery. I'm visiting with my daughter. No nurse has even been in here to help me shower."

The Queen of Ice barely stopped to catch her breath.

"Do you know that the woman who shot me was, at one time, my loving husband's mistress? Now, you go think that over. And in about thirty minutes, send another nurse in here to help me shower. You stay out!"

Sadie turned her back on the nurse and the nurse left the room.

Sadie turned to Savannah. "I'll never forgive you for not letting me kill him."

This time Savannah laughed.

"I'm kinda sorry I stopped you. Well, this is my cue to go home, shower, see my husband and your grandchildren. I'll be back shortly.

"You've got a slew of people, other than Buddy, waiting outside to see you and hear all you have to say. And obviously, that's going to keep you busy for a while."

Sadie took a deep breath and let out a string of her favorite swear words.

"They had better figure out a way to keep that son-of-a-bitch away from me. I don't like him, honey girl."

"I'm beginning to get that, Mama. You don't hide it well, at all."

"Really? Even in front of the people outside the realm?"

"Mama, even the Governor knows you hate Buddy at this point. You haven't said much in the last few days, but, what you have said, you've said loudly.

"Now, try to behave. I'll be back. I can see that you're going to be just fine." Savannah assured her mother.

"You go spend time with Beau and the babies. The next time I see you, I want you to have those babies with you, and I want to be able to hold them." Sadie instructed.

Savannah kissed her mother and left. She hated leaving her, they did have good drugs here, but she sure missed being at home. She turned around to look at her mother again. Sadie smiled at her. The same smile Savannah had seen a million times, just like nothing had ever happened.

"Mama, you're crazy. But I sure as hell wouldn't have it any other way."

Caroline was in the waiting room when Savannah came out. "Should I go in?" Caroline asked.

"I think you'd better. Buddy was demanding to see her a little while ago and Mama is really mad because no one killed him for her while she was unconscious. She blames us, Caroline."

"She's okay then." Caroline laughed as she hugged Savannah and headed for Sadie's room.

As usual, she was interrupted by a detective. "I need to go in with you, Mrs. Harrington. We need to hear everything Mrs. Montgomery says.

"Her accusations regarding Sally Blevins aren't really plausible. We need to know why she believes it was Sally Blevins who shot her and we need to try to find out if she remembers anything else."

Sadie stuck to her story. Her memory was very clear on Sally Blevins screaming at her "You Bitch" then pointing a gun and shooting her. Sally was standing beside her navy blue Explorer.

"If you want to keep coming in here and going over this shit, I'll check myself out of here. You'll not have access to me in my own home.

"Weren't ya'll standing out there? Didn't any of you see her? You were almost as close to her as I was. Why the hell didn't you see anything? Caroline, how did you manage to avoid seeing her?"

"We did hear her yell, we heard the shot, but we were all looking at you. She jumped in the car and took off. We didn't get the license plate number because it had something over it and we couldn't see it.

"Mrs. Montgomery, we've been doing everything we can. But we can't search her car and her home without probable cause."

At that moment, Buddy burst into Sadie's room.

"Sadie, you have got to stop accusing Sally of shooting you." The Senator was begging.

"Well, pardon the hell out of me! Should I not have mentioned I saw your ex-lover as she called me a bitch, pointed a gun at me and pulled the trigger? Tough shit, Buddy! It was her, and the bitch shot me, nearly killed me. That's all, pal! Get out of here!"

The Senator was still pleading. "Sadie, you're just trying to punish her for what happened in the past. She's a good woman. She's not capable of killing anyone."

"Well, listen to you. So protective of your mousey little ex-mistress.

"Oh, for crying out loud! You're still having an affair with her!"

Sadie looked at the detective.

"There's your probable cause. Go get her ass."

"NO, don't." Buddy said.

Sadie stood up, shakily. "Get the fuck out of my room!" Sadie jerked the cord for the nurse several times. The nursing staff was very uncomfortable over the situation, but Sadie was the loudest. They came and escorted Buddy back to his room.

Sadie then lit into the detective before he could get out of the room.

"Why in hell aren't you at her house? Find the gun. Find the bullets. They're going to match up. She was trying to kill me when she shot Buddy by mistake. Am I going to have to go to her house and make a citizen's arrest or are you guys going to go get her?"

The detective was stunned. He knew she was right.

However, the Senator had practically threatened to have all of their jobs if they pursued the investigation of Sally Blevins. In either shooting.

They had discovered the affair between the Senator and Sally Blevins was ongoing. It had started a few years back. Sally's husband had divorced her, naming the Senator in an alienation of affection suit. The affair kept up and it appeared Sadie was unaware of it. The next step was to search Sally's house for the gun. But she would have to be an idiot not to have gotten rid of it.

They were putting off the search warrant because of pressure from the Senator.

Now they were getting pressure from Sadie to find the gun. They were sure Sadie was right. It was just a matter of time. Maybe the time was now. Sadie was demanding action.

Suddenly, Sadie came up with just what she needed to get them moving. She threatened to call a news conference and declare the authorities were not investigating Sally because she had been the Senator's mistress for years. And she added that she was sure the detective had seen her friend Jim Wilson in the waiting room. Sadie would be summoning him to be her next visitor.

"I'm ashamed to say this, but you all know I'll photograph well, and I will draw one hell of an audience. Everyone will tune in to see me and hear what I'm going to say. This is a threat, detective."

Okay. The time had arrived. They had to serve the warrant.

As the detective turned to go, Sadie smiled at him.

"If you can prove the Senator was in on the plot to kill me, I'll give you a very nice piece from my jewelry collection."

The detective couldn't help but laugh as he went out the door. And he did try to help it.

19

The Senator was finally going to be discharged, but he wouldn't go home. He kept finding little aches and pains to ensure his stay. He was going nowhere as long as Sadie was there. He could always complain about a headache and get some attention.

The bandages on his head had long since been taken off. He claimed weakness, but he got around fine. He paced impatiently between his room and the I.C.U. where Sadie was being kept. He was constantly trying to get into Sadie's room when he saw a detective going in to speak with her.

Sadie was bandaged from beneath her arms to her waist. They were changing the bandages regularly and assured her she was healing well. She was still weak and could not walk without some dizziness. It was taking her a while to regain her strength.

Dr. McKenzie wasn't anywhere close to dismissing her. He wouldn't even let her be moved from the protected I.C.U. into a private room.

The gossip and drama taking place in the hospital was so heavy you would think Buddy and Sadie were the only patients there.

Sadie feigned some sort of malady every time Buddy tried to come in to see her. He had crossed the line when he had burst in to protect Sally.

Sadie only wanted to see Savannah, Beau and the babies and Caroline.

The days dragged on. But the criminal officials were busy and making great progress.

The silly bitch hadn't gotten rid of the gun. Her fingerprints were all over it and—*oh, my*! What a surprise! The bullets matched.

Buddy was finally discharged from the hospital. He was spending some of his time at the Capitol, but most of his time with Sally Blevins' attorney. He really didn't want her charged with attempted murder. And was trying to do all he could to help her. But a week later she was charged. And Buddy had paid her bail. Sadie was in a rage. She now refused to let Buddy's calls come through.

Sadie couldn't seem to regain her strength. Savannah had come to sit with her for a while—or rather—nap on the bed beside her. They were resting quietly, both drifting in and out of a light sleep.

Sadie said softly, "Are you awake, honey?"

"Yes, Mama. Do you need anything?"

"I need to tell you that I want to be the voice in your head always telling you that you are loved, you are wonderful and smart and funny. And you can do anything.

"Instead, I'm afraid all you'll remember is 'Brush your teeth, wash your face, and be sure to check your makeup'.

"That's not fair to me. It's not how I want you to remember me. I want you to cherish my memory. Oh, God! Savannah, don't cry! That's what you'll remember about me.

You'll hate me for always making you cry. Why do you hate me? I've tried to understand what I did to cause that."

Sadie's head fell to the side of her pillow. She was exhausted. Her eyes were closed. She appeared to be out like a light. Savannah cried softly as she watched her mother.

"I'll remember it all, Mama." Savannah said quietly. She wondered if her mother was asleep, or just letting her latest words marinate in Savannah's brain. Why am I so suspicious of her? Has she ever done anything but show me love and devotion? There's just something about her that makes me feel as though I had left her back at that farm and that I'm responsible for all the things that happened to her at that damned place. Or some such shit! "I don't understand why you feel that way, either, Mama."

Savannah's mind drifted off until she was quietly awakened by the nurse taking her mother's vital signs.

"Is she okay?" Savannah asked in a whisper.

"She seems to be, but she's still awfully weak. She needs to rest, but she can't seem to."

"No." Savannah agreed. "She feels if she sleeps, things will happen without her supervision."

The nurse smiled at Savannah.

"She seems like a good woman. I've heard nothing but praise for her." The nurse was still smiling at Savannah as she walked out of the room.

"Thank you." Savannah said softly to the nurse after she had left the room. Is everybody paid to lay this guilt trip on me, you smug little bitch?

Savannah turned back toward her mother to resume her bedside vigil as her mother slept.

The day came for Sadie's dismissal from the hospital.

That bastard Buddy showed up to drive her home. He had parked his car behind Savannah's in the Patient Dismissal lane. Sadie's car was already at the hospital, in the visitor's parking lot. It had been there for a while.

Sadie told Savannah to go on home. But first, she needed to talk to Buddy, then she would drive her own car home.

"Oh I don't think so, lady. You can barely walk unassisted. You are weak as a kitten. You are not going to drive your own car anywhere. I have given Beau the keys and he'll pick your car up from the parking lot. Go on and talk to Buddy. I'll wait"

Sadie was used to Savannah's bossy ways. She would let it slide as she knew she had no business driving a car in her weakened condition.

She was incensed by having to be wheeled out of the hospital. She had no choice, so she had the nurse wheel her to Buddy's car.

Sadie got into the passenger's seat of the Senator's car and closed the door.

"You are *not* coming back to my house. Don't you dare start this car, Senator. I know how hard you are working to try to keep the bitch who tried to kill me—twice—from paying for it. I know when you got shot, it was intended for me. I know you bailed her out of jail.

"I'll see you both on death row, if I can manage it." The hatred bounced all around inside the car.

Buddy rolled down his window to let some of it out. He had broken out into a sweat.

Savannah got out of her car and went to Buddy's when she saw the tale tell signs that she had seen so many times before, indicating that her mother and step-father were "having words." Sadie had rolled her window down by now and Savannah could hear their conversation.

Buddy was going pale.

"Is the guilt getting to you, Buddy? Or is it just worry over Sally's predicament?"

Sadie's voice was soft now. "You won't get by with any of this, neither will your little Sally. You should have never done that to your best friend. I don't give a shit that you did it to me. I'm finished with you."

Buddy seemed to be having trouble breathing. David was standing by the car, just a couple of feet beyond Savannah.

Sadie turned and called to David. "You need to get him some help. I think he's ill."

Then she turned back to Buddy. Cold and hard. "You're out of my life, you son-of-a-bitch. Out of it for good. You have no excuse for being such a worthless, lying bastard."

The Senator's head had dropped to his chest and his body slumped in his seat. She saw David and a couple of the medical staff running toward them with a gurney.

Sadie got out of the car and watched as they loaded Buddy onto the gurney. Sadie turned to her daughter. "I'm sorry, Savannah. Stay with him if you want to. I have something I have to take care of right now."

Savannah grabbed Sadie's hand and they walked toward the gurney which was carrying Buddy back into the hospital. The attendant was desperately trying to find a pulse. "He's gone" the attendant said matter-of-factly. The attendants were almost running with the gurney now.

Savannah and Sadie stopped and hugged each other. Savannah was crying softly. Over the last couple of months, Savannah had watched her step-father turn into a demanding brute. She realized he had always been that way with her mother. Then she had discovered he had had a mistress for years. That woman had shot her mother. Right up to the last, Buddy was protecting his mistress. He was not the man she had wanted him to be. She would find it hard to grieve for him.

She turned to see her mother talking with her step-father's staff. Most likely already instructing them to make the appropriate arrangements for the announcement of his death and for the funeral.

20

The Senator was pronounced dead soon after entering the emergency room. They had worked on him for about twenty minutes, but they knew it was useless from the start.

Sadie told David which funeral home to use and asked him to call the Episcopal priest to make arrangements.

"Have the priest arrange services to his preference. He can call me if need be.

"You call me if you need me for anything. You have my cell number. I will attend his funeral, but not as his widow. I want no mention of me in the service. This is all about the Senator—just like it always was. They will probably want his body to lie in state in the Rotunda for a day. Do what you think he would want. I'll be in touch later."

Then Sadie and Savannah got into Savannah's car. "I need to go home first, baby, then we need to go to the bank and I have to get into Buddy's lock box."

They got to Sadie's house and Savannah following her directly to the Senator's study and to his desk. Sadie quickly broke into the locked drawer and found the key to his lock box, just what she was looking for. "This is it, let's go to the bank."

Savannah drove like a bat out of hell to the bank. They gained access to Buddy's lock box and both of them nearly fainted.

Savannah and Sadie gasped and looked at each other in shock. As Sadie picked up each item, she handed it to Savannah to inspect. They were silent as they searched through the treasures.

There was so much cash, they were afraid to count it. Marriage license and divorce decree to some woman in Europe. A beautifully wrapped box—apparently not meant for Sadie. She opened it. An enormous square cut emerald surrounded by diamonds. My God! She tried her fingers until she found one it fit. Ring finger—left hand. Sorry, tacky as it was, wedding ring got dropped in her purse and emerald went on. Too soon? Not for Senator Buddy's widow. Savannah stared wide-eyed. "Who was supposed to have that?"

"I'm guessing it was meant for Sally."

"If you think it's in bad taste, Mama, I can wear it." Savannah generously offered.

"You'll have it one day. Oh, I'll have my engagement ring reset to your liking. How's that, baby?"

"It'll do, I guess." Savannah was smiling.

His Will, which Sadie had forced him to make two weeks after they married, was there. Her prayer was he had not made another, but under the circumstances, she could have a new one over-thrown due to influence by the would-be assassin, Sally.

Sadie emptied out the lock box. It included the Deed for the house, in both their names. Guess who had it all to herself? Thank you Sweet Jesus!

Sadie realized she must seem like a cold hearted harpy. Don't we all agree he deserved it? She told herself.

They gathered everything up and left the bank.

Sadie and Savannah talked all the way on the drive back to Sadie's house about the bizarre events of the last few months.

Sadie apologized to Savannah and Savannah apologized to Sadie. Then they cried a little over Buddy's death. Then they spoke wide-eyed about the findings in the lock box.

"How much money do you think is in there, Mama?"

"Far more than I dreamed of, but not nearly what I've earned."

Sadie read the Will again when she got home. Two hefty insurance policies and several property deeds. Lots of money. Plus the stash in the lock box: $400,000.00 in cash. Savannah refused to leave until it was all counted and recounted. Where the hell had that come from? No need to mention that to anyone else. She would be a good girl and not expose him to the authorities. There would be enough ugliness. She would hold back on the cash money, and the ring.

Savannah said she would go home and take care of some things and be right back. She kissed Sadie and they had a long hug. Sadie watched her leave and went back into the house.

She walked through her home. Such peace and tranquility. She looked out at her yard. Outside of the sun room, were three new huge glorious gardenia bushes that hadn't been there before. So this was the surprise her neighbor, Bridgette O'Shay, had planted for Sadie while she was at the hospital.

Sadie went to her sun porch and lay down to rest. God, what a day. She must have drifted off to sleep when she was awakened by a noise.

Sadie saw Savannah, Beau and the kids drive into the driveway. Right behind them was Caroline and Wagner. They got out of the car, unloading food. Oh, Lord have mercy. Here come the mourners and the funeral food.

Oh hell! Was the kitchen clean? Next came Bridgette driving up. She must be loaded down with food and drink or she wouldn't have driven such a short distance.

Sadie wouldn't have to explain not having called anyone. She was the queen of inappropriate actions. Even Caroline would cut her some slack.

Sadie noticed that Savannah wasn't even crying. Sadly, the Senator had really shown his bad side over the last month of his life. Gossip was still rampant that Buddy and Sally were planning the demise of Sadie.

Sadie no longer cared how much Buddy was involved. Good old Sally was putting all the blame on Buddy. She would have been such a devoted wife if the assassination attempt had worked. Now she was sullying Buddy's name to an extent even Sadie wouldn't have gone. Of course, Sadie's life wasn't on the line—any more.

Okay, Sadie. Back to the present.

No need to worry about the kitchen. Bridgette and Caroline would take care of covering for her if the kitchen wasn't sparkling.

Robert and Eve Roper, Beau's parents, arrived next. These good, dignified people whom Sadie loved dearly, had been relegated to 'Pap and Swooze', the full-time baby sitters since Sadie had been shot.

Sadie pulled both of them close to her.

"Thank you so much for caring for our sweet babies all this time." Sadie whispered.

"Of course," Robert said as he returned her hug.

"Well, you're up off your ass now, so it's your turn." Eve teased as she hugged Sadie. "You know we loved every minute of it—just hated the circumstances. Are you going to be all right, lady?"

"Better than ever." Sadie smiled at both of them. "I've missed you both. We'll get together for some fun later."

How lucky, thought Sadie. I even like my daughter's in-laws. We are a strange family.

Then, it was car after car coming into her driveway. Remember? You're in the South. Death brings food and people. Sadie wasn't up to having hundreds of people traipsing through her home.

She hurried into the kitchen, relieved it was spotless. Caroline and Bridgette had taken over. Neither of them having to ask where the good linens, china and silver were located.

They began to prepare the tables and accept the food as it was brought in. Everyone looked sort of familiar to Sadie. Politicians, church folk and good friends. Soon the house was full. Most everyone had brought liquor along with food. Good thinking.

No one mentioned the outrageously large emerald surrounded by diamonds Sadie was suddenly wearing on her wedding ring finger. She wondered what she would say if anyone did mention it. Most probably her answer would be inappropriate.

She watched as the tables and the dining and living rooms began to fill with food and people. Everyone was hugging her and telling her how sorry they were.

When someone Sadie didn't like hugged her, and she knew they were being phony, Sadie would gasp and moan loudly when they touched her. Just a little reminder she was still recovering from a near death experience herself. She knew she was being cruel and embarrassing the person, but what the hell. They had been sticking up for little ole Sally and chances were, they had brought one of those awful molded fruit salads. She intended to find out what her enemies had brought, so she could rail about it later to Caroline and prove how tacky they were.

No, Sadie would not see the irony in how tacky she was being in judging who brought what funeral food. Southerners were allowed to be judgmental regarding such things. Weren't they? Well, Sadie was.

Under the most unusual circumstances of this particular death, many people were just there to gawk. Sadie did notice some uniformed security milling about. She went out to them, personally, and carried plates of food. She had a special table set up for them on the patio and made sure liquor was available to the ones who weren't so strait-laced about drinking on the job.

Sadie actually preferred being outside on the patio with them, so she made many unnecessary trips out there and stayed longer than was fitting.

There were many people who just drove up to pay their respects. Good country people who never knew the Senator, but knew he was a good Senator and looked out for the people. Sadie didn't know them, but she went out to their cars and thanked them and sent covered paper plates of food home with them. She also sent food home with the security men as they changed shifts. To those who knew Sadie best, it was obvious she would do anything to get away from the throngs inside.

At one point, Sadie, Caroline and Brigette were discussing the enormous turnout of people. It didn't matter whether they were there to show respect or just out of curiosity. Sadie had remarked that she couldn't get this big a turnout if she had shot herself and took half of Louisiana with her. She was properly shushed by Caroline amid badly chosen giggles and outright hooting and hollering from the men.

This visiting and story telling went on into the late evening. The guests were thinning out until only the closest friends of Sadie's and political cronies of Buddy remained.

Most of the cronies were too drunk to know it was time to go home. They were telling story after story of Buddy's political prowess. Some of them were so drunk, they were telling stories of his sexual escapades. Too drunk to realize they could be insulting his widow, the hostess.

Sadie had decided to have the security men haul their asses off when she got tired of them, which was about midnight.

Finally, it was just Sadie, Savannah and her family, Bridgette, Caroline and Wagner. The babies were asleep upstairs. Caroline, Wagner and Bridgette were cleaning up and visiting quietly, winding down as they cleaned the kitchen and the rest of the house.

Sadie did let her mind drift for a moment to how very pleased Buddy would have been at the huge turnout. He had missed out on a hell of a drunk. But it was the only one she could recall him missing out on.

When the house was back in order, they gathered up the food and Bridgette volunteered her assistant to have it delivered to homeless shelters throughout town the next morning.

Everything settled, Bridgette, Caroline and Wagner hugged Sadie and said their good-byes.

Only Savannah and Beau and the babies remained. Sadie insisted Catherine Virginia and Roger Montgomery sleep over. She would deliver them sometime tomorrow, or probably

Savannah should come and pick them up. Sadie probably shouldn't drive for a couple of days.

As Sadie walked through the house and to her favorite sun room, she felt light as a feather.

Savannah had followed her.

"This has been a horror, Mama. Do you need to talk about anything?"

Sadie sat on the bed and pulled Savannah to her.

"You and that brood of yours, are my reason for living. Thanks for sticking with me during my death watch. Things will be better now."

Savannah's eye suddenly caught sight of the ring on Sadie's finger.

"Good Lord, Mama! That thing is huge! Don't you just love it? I know you must feel awkward wearing it."

"Get over yourself, kid. Let's pretend it was intended for me. It would be in total bad taste for Sally to wear it in prison. I will, of course, attend Buddy's funeral. Then, no more talk of him. I finally got rid of one.

"No! Not a word of criticism. I don't deserve it and I'm too rich now to tolerate it. You and Caroline have an assignment. I'm never to re-marry. This house and the money are all mine— ours.

"No more bullying from Buddy or any man. My affairs will only be shallow ones with very young men.

"Now, you, Beau and the kids can go on with your everyday activities. You don't have to baby-sit me anymore. Maybe next week you can come over and help me rid myself and this house of things we don't need or want."

Sadie hugged and kissed Beau. Then Sadie and Savannah hugged, kissed and declared their undying love for one another—until...Oh, let's not dwell.

As Sadie watched them drive down the street, she turned to look at her favorite room.

She walked into the bedroom part of the sun room. She folded her arms and leaned against the door frame. As she gazed at the beautiful Moroccan cover on the daybed, the warm rich colors on the walls and the exotic décor of the room, she sighed deeply.

"Bless your heart, darlin'." she said aloud to herself, "You may get that good night's sleep, after all."